TASHA'S PROBLEM

"I see you ignored my advice and registered for the mathematics examination," Mr. Cala declared. "Do you realize that you could harm the reputation of the school?"

Tasha held back the words she really wanted to say. She just stared at him.

"It's a shame you young women never choose to meet a challenge properly."

"Excuse me, Mr. Cala," Tasha said. "Just what do you mean, *you young women never—*"

"Fathers train their sons to meet challenges forcefully," Mr. Cala said without hesitation. "It's not your fault. It is a matter of your upbringing."

Tasha felt her shoulders tighten.

"Mr. Cala," Tasha replied, trying to remain calm, "I'm meeting this challenge the way my *father* taught me to meet anything—head-on."

18 Pine St.

The Test

Written by
Stacie Johnson

Created by
WALTER DEAN MYERS

A Seth Godin Production

BANTAM BOOKS
NEW YORK · TORONTO · LONDON · SYDNEY · AUCKLAND

RL 5, age 10 and up

THE TEST
A Bantam Book / January 1993

Special thanks to Judy Gitenstein, Betsy Gould, Amy Berkower, Fran Lebowitz, Linda Lannon, Michael Cader, Alex Simmons, Margery Mandell, José Arroyo, Kate Grossman, Helene Godin, and Lucy Wood.

18 Pine St. is a trademark of Seth Godin Productions, Inc.

ISBN 0-553-29722-8

Published simultaneously in the United States and Canada

PRINTED IN THE UNITED STATES OF AMERICA

RAD 0 9 8 7 6 5 4 3 2 1

For Lisa Orden Zarin

18 Pine St.

There was a card shop at 8 Pine Street, and a shop that sold sewing supplies at 10 Pine that was only open in the afternoons and on Saturdays if it didn't rain. For some reason that no one seemed to know or care about, there was no 12, 14, or 16 Pine. The name of the pizzeria at 18 Pine Street had been Antonio's before Mr. and Mrs. Harris took it over. Mr. Harris had taken down Antonio's sign and just put up a sign announcing the address. By the time he got around to thinking of a name for the place, everybody was calling it 18 Pine.

The Crew at 18 Pine St.

Sarah Gordon is the heart and soul of the group. Sarah's pretty, with a great smile and a warm, caring attitude that makes her a terrific friend. Sarah's the reason that everyone shows up at 18 Pine St.

Tasha Gordon, tall, sexy, and smart, is Sarah's cousin. Since her parents died four years ago, Tasha has moved from relative to relative. Now she's living with Sarah and her family—maybe for good.

Cindy Phillips is Sarah's best friend. Cindy is petite, with dark, radiant skin and a cute nose. She wears her black hair in braids. Cindy's been Sarah's neighbor and friend since she moved from Jamaica when she was three.

Kwame Brown's only a sophomore, but that doesn't stop him from being part of the crew. Kwame's got a flattop haircut, black-framed glasses, and mischievous smile. As the smartest kid in the group, he's the one Jennifer turns to for help with her homework.

Jennifer Wilson is the poor little rich girl. Her parents are divorced, and all the charge cards and clothes in the world can't make up for it. Jennifer's tall and thin, with cocoa-colored skin and a body that's made for all those designer clothes she wears.

Billy Turner is a basketball star. His good looks, sharp clothes, and thin mustache make him a star with the women as well. He's already broken Sarah's heart—and now Tasha's got her eyes on him as well.

April Winter has been to ten schools in the last ten years—and she hopes she's at Murphy to stay. Her energy, blond hair, and offbeat personality make her a standout at school.

Brian Wu is a math wizard. A good friend of Kwame's, Brian's always happy to help him with the latest project.

And there's Dave Hunter, José Melendez, and the rest of the gang. You'll meet them all in the halls of Murphy High and after school for a pizza at 18 Pine St.

One

"Dad's trying to burn the house down!" Allison Gordon yelled as she backed out of the kitchen. A moment later, her cousin Tasha was standing beside her, looking over her shoulder.

A cloud of gray smoke filled the kitchen and stung their eyes.

Mr. Gordon, Tasha's uncle, had just plunged a four-quart pot into the sink and turned on the tap. The rushing water sent up a cloud of steam as Mr. Gordon tried not to burn his hands.

Allison grabbed a towel and fanned the smoke away from her. "Leave the door open," she yelled.

Sarah Gordon appeared at the door and rushed over to her father at the sink. "What happened?" She looked

1

down at the pot. The contents were an unidentifiable mass of blackened lumps and bits.

"Dinner?" Tasha asked as she crossed to the stove and turned on the overhead vent.

"It was"—her uncle nodded—"ten minutes ago."

"Donald, you didn't burn your mother's Bijou stew?" Mrs. Gordon entered the room and hurried over to the sink.

"Technically," Mr. Gordon said with a sigh, "the fire burned the stew. I'm sort of acting as damage control."

"Miss Essie asked Dad to watch the stew while she ran to the store for some kind of spice," Allison told the others. "But he fell asleep at the TV and—"

"And where were you?" Mr. Gordon interrupted Allison.

"I was doing my homework," his younger daughter said, using her best angelic manner. "Just like you told me to."

"She's got you there, Uncle Donald." Tasha smiled.

"It would have been helpful if you two had come home from school early for once," Mr. Gordon said. He tried to look stern, but his smile gave him away. "After all, I'm not very good at these—"

Mrs. Gordon eyed her husband suspiciously. "Are you implying that cooking is *women's* work?"

Mr. Gordon raised his hands in a gesture of surrender. "I wouldn't think of such a thing. Especially being outnumbered five to one."

"A wise move," Mrs. Gordon replied, smiling.

Tasha couldn't help smiling, too. She sat on the stool

and crossed her long legs at the ankles. She had seen the Gordons play this game before. Though she had only recently come to live with her father's brother and his family, Mr. and Mrs. Gordon had welcomed her with open arms. Miss Essie, her grandmother, had proved to be a strong and caring force in the household. And Sarah's eleven-year-old sister, Allison, was like a sister to Tasha—adorable one minute, a pain the next.

But Tasha's relationship with Sarah had taken the most effort to form, and had proved to be the most precious. Sarah had slightly darker skin than Tasha and layered black hair that curved stylishly behind her ears.

Sarah was different from her cousin in many ways. Tasha was athletic, flamboyant, and flirtatious, while Sarah was quieter, though she had dozens of friends and a knack for making people feel comfortable. They often disagreed, but Sarah was as close to Tasha as anyone could be. With each passing day they were becoming less like cousins and more like sisters.

"I'm sorry we were late, Dad," Sarah said. "Tasha and I went to 18 Pine after school. Everybody was there and—"

"We lost track of time, talking," Tasha finished for her.

18 Pine St. was the best pizza parlor in town and the favorite hangout for most of the kids from Murphy High School. Almost every afternoon since she had come to live with the Gordons, Tasha had joined Sarah and their friends for after-school sodas and pizzas. It was almost a ritual, a time to recover from the day

before going home to face parents and homework.

"What was so fascinating," Mr. Gordon asked, as they began cleaning up the mess, "that you left me to cremate dinner?"

"Boys," Sarah replied. "The care and feeding of them in the wild habitat of Murphy High."

"You make them sound as if they're not civilized," Mr. Gordon said as he poured the water out of the burned pot.

"I have serious reservations about the ability of any boy to be completely civilized," Tasha said. "They start off pulling your hair when you're in the first grade and end up burning up your pots!"

"Ouch!" Mr. Gordon said, wincing.

"We going to order pizza for dinner?" Allison asked.

"I think we can rescue part of the dinner," Mr. Gordon said as he checked the other pots on the stove. "The room is airing out, and the worst of it is over."

Just then they heard the front door slam, and a moment later Miss Essie walked into the room. She was a heavyset woman with chestnut-colored skin and twinkling brown eyes.

"I found the tarragon I needed for the—" Miss Essie's friendly smile froze as she noticed the still-smoky kitchen and the pot in her son's hands.

"Well," Mr. Gordon said sheepishly, "maybe the worst is yet to come."

"Would you pass another slice?" Allison asked her mother. "This time with pepperoni on it."

The Gordons sat around the kitchen table laughing and talking. The remnants of a large pizza lay in the center of the table, along with several two-liter bottles of soda.

"That's wasn't so bad," Mr. Gordon said as he popped the last of his slice into his mouth.

Miss Essie eyed him. "Compared to charcoal briskets of beef with deep-scorched gravy, this was a banquet."

Mr. Gordon placed his hand on her shoulder. "Will you ever forgive me, Mother?"

"Of course I will," Miss Essie replied, then muttered, "in my next life." She grinned and everyone laughed. "By the way, Tasha, there's a letter for you on the kitchen counter." Miss Essie pointed with the serving fork.

Tasha reached back and picked up the amber-colored envelope. "It's from Shareen Aldridge," she exclaimed. "Shareen was one of my best friends back in Oakland."

"How come she hasn't written you before this?" Allison asked.

Tasha grinned. "Shareen would spend hours overdressing to go to the corner store. She'd talk on the phone forever, and she'd hang out in the local mall for days, boy-watching and window-shopping. But write a letter—she'd rather have a tooth pulled."

"So what prompted her to endure such torture for you this time?" Sarah teased.

"I'll let you know in a minute." Tasha began reading the letter.

"What does it say?" Allison asked, trying to peek.

"I thought we'd taught you better about respecting people's privacy," Mr. Gordon said. A sly smile spread across his face. "Of course, if Tasha *wants* to share her correspondence with—"

"Donald!" Mrs. Gordon exclaimed, laughing. "How could you?"

"Blame it on my home environment," Mr. Gordon replied. "I'm married to a fact-finding lawyer, and I have two sharp, intuitive daughters who—"

"And you have a job that requires you to snoop on the affairs of over five hundred hyperactive teenagers," Mrs. Gordon said cheerfully. Mr. Gordon was the principal at the town's alternative high school, Hamilton.

"My dad," Allison cheered, "principal of I Spy High."

There was a smattering of chuckles before the room fell silent.

Tasha looked up from the amber-colored pages to find everyone staring at her, including Miss Essie. "All right, all right," she said. "I'll read it to you. *'Dear Tosh, Time flies, girl. You haven't been gone that long, but it seems like forever. I can tell you now, good gossip sisters are hard to find. And no one could scope boys better than'* " ... Tasha stopped reading and eyed the family with a hint of embarrassment on her face. "She's exaggerating ... kind of."

"Right," Sarah said sarcastically. She exchanged a grin with her cousin. "It's okay. You can skip the juicy parts until Little Ears"—she nodded toward Allison—

"has gone to bed."

Allison made a sour face at her older sister.

Tasha skipped a few lines, then continued. " *'I'm sure you've got it all under control there in Madison. You always were the one in the spotlight.'* " Tasha looked up at Sarah. After the success of the Romeo Rap, their junior class fund raiser, it was her cousin who was basking in the spotlight, not her.

" *'Anyway, I guess you're shocked to hear from me,'* " Tasha continued. " *'Frankly, I'm surprised, myself. But my parents were talking about how things are changing around here, who has moved in, who's moved out, and well...we started talking about you and your folks.'* " Tasha hesitated. " *'My mother remembered that it has been almost four years since your parents died in that car accident.'* "

Tasha looked up in time to catch the same expression of uneasiness on everyone's face. They all knew that the anniversary of the day when her parents had died was coming up in two weeks. But none of them had said a word about it.

Tasha had no way of knowing that Mr. and Mrs. Gordon had discussed it several times already, trying to decide how they might observe the day, now that Tasha was with them.

Miss Essie had suggested a family visit to the church, but no one had mentioned that to Tasha yet. Tasha had never attended church with the family before. She spent Sunday morning running or sleeping.

And Tasha hadn't felt any reason to bring up the matter until now. "It's all right," she said with a slight edge to her voice. "I dealt with my parents' death a long time ago. It's no big deal."

"Are you sure?" Sarah asked. She hadn't known her football-star uncle very well because he and her own father hadn't been very close. Sarah knew that Tasha had adored him, even though his career hadn't left him much time for his family.

Tasha felt a knot forming in her stomach. "Trust me, cousin," she replied as she folded up the letter. "I'm capable of doing a lot of things, even without your helping hand."

Tasha wasn't certain why Sarah's question had irritated her so. Maybe it was that Sarah was always trying to mother her, and that was something Tasha hated in the worst way. It had been the sore spot that set them against each other when they first met. But that was over now... or was it?

"I think I'll read the rest of this letter in private."

"I have some after-dinner business to take care of, too," Mr. Gordon said, trying to change the subject. "The math competition is next weekend, and I have some kids who want to take it."

"What math competition?" Allison asked.

"It's a major-league county-wide math contest for kids who are really good in algebra, trig, and geometry," Sarah explained, glad to move the conversation away from her cousin. "It's an all-day thing and the winners get some sort of scholarships. Right, Dad?"

"That's right," her father replied. "Since Hamilton

kids are considered students with extreme hardships or learning difficulties, it's important for me to be supportive of any young person who wants to enter an academic competition."

"Are there any kids from Madison High entering the contest?" Miss Essie asked.

"I'm sure all the real brains are," Sarah answered.

Her grandmother raised an eyebrow. "But not you?"

"Math isn't my strong point," Sarah was sorry to have to admit. "I guess I picked up your genes for show business, Miss Essie, not my parents' academic skills."

"You can do anything you set your mind to, Sarah," Mrs. Gordon said. "You know that."

"There's really not enough time to prepare for the competition," Sarah replied. "I'm afraid the Gordon family won't be represented this year."

"Maybe it will," Tasha said suddenly. "I have a good grade average in math." She turned toward Sarah. "Maybe I'll enter the contest."

"Tasha, get real!" Sarah said in surprise. "You're on the basketball team, the soccer team and—"

"That hasn't stopped me from getting good grades before," Tasha said, cutting Sarah off. "In Oakland I was a lot more active—in a number of ways."

"Why not give it a try?" Mr. Gordon said.

"Who do I see to enter?" Tasha asked.

"Mr. Cala, probably," Sarah said. "He's the math teacher."

"Then Mr. Cala will see me in the morning," Tasha said.

9

PINE

Two

Murphy High was an old-fashioned building. It extended over an entire block, dominated by a wide porch with columns. An ivory-trimmed brick structure with a rolling front lawn, it dominated the view for blocks along Eastmont Avenue.

Tasha had been impressed with the school from the very first time she saw it. It was different from the modern steel and glass high school she'd gone to in Oakland, California. Murphy seemed to come with a life of its own—a rich history and long corridors of ancient secrets.

Now, as Tasha hurried with Sarah and Cindy Phillips toward the building, there was a damp chill in the morning air. A misty rain fell from a steel-gray sky. It felt more like a dreary Monday than two days before the weekend.

Kids strolled or raced into the school, chatting about dates, parents, and overdue assignments. Sarah and Cindy stopped on the steps to talk about a new guy Cindy had noticed.

"So what else have you learned about him, besides his vital statistics?" Tasha heard Sarah ask.

"The boy has the body of a honey-coated god," Cindy purred. "What more do I need to know?"

"A lot more," Sarah replied. "If you know what I mean."

Since her brief romance with a boy named Ibrahim Zahid, Sarah's best friend had taken a new attitude toward dating. When Tasha had first met her, Cindy had been reluctant to get involved with anyone. Then Ibrahim, a student from Africa, who claimed to be a prince, had entered the picture. For a while, Cindy had become lost in him, and her behavior had thrown her into a major clash with her friends.

But in the end, the romance had failed, and Tasha and Sarah had discovered that Ibrahim had been hiding a darker secret than any of them had suspected.

Cindy had been deeply hurt, but instead of retreating, she seemed to be coming on stronger. Perhaps it was all the love and support she received from Sarah and Tasha, as well as her other friends Jennifer Wilson

12

and April Winter. Or, Tasha suspected, Cindy was simply a lot tougher than any of them had guessed.

"Oh, let her have a good time, *Mama* Gordon," Tasha kidded. "If he's a bum, she can dump him, and we'll help."

"And if he's a dream?" Sarah left the question hanging.

Tasha smiled wickedly. "Then we'll steal him from her!" She raced through the front doors with Cindy and Sarah close behind.

"You just try it!" Cindy said, laughing as they stopped in the crowded hall.

"Seriously," Tasha said. "I wish you all the luck." She brushed a long lock of curly hair out of her eyes. "Now I've got to get to class."

"Are you going to see Mr. Cala first thing?" Sarah asked.

"I think I'll wait until third period," Tasha replied. "I have him for math anyway."

"Good luck," Cindy said. "Mr. Cala isn't known for his smooth talk and sparkling disposition."

Tasha winked. "I can handle it."

The three girls said their good-byes and melted into the rushing stream of students.

Tasha had once said that listening to Mr. Cala talking was like playing a damaged heavy-metal album at full volume. Unfortunately, Mr. Cala had overheard that remark, and since then their relationship had been tense, to say the least.

The math teacher, who also was the assistant head of the math department, had a loud, grating voice which seemed to pierce right through a student. And when he yelled at someone, it was even more unbearable.

Tasha studied him as he paced around the room, trying to choose the best way to approach him. For most of the period he talked on and on about ratios and trigonometric theorems. His hands barely reached to clasp behind his huge frame, and his watery brown eyes squinted through his tortoiseshell glasses. Occasionally he massaged his scalp through his medium Afro, speckled with gray.

When the bell rang, Tasha figured it was now or never. She intercepted him at the classroom door. "Excuse me, Mr. Cala," she said. He was, as always, neatly dressed, and Tasha noticed the heavy smell of tobacco smoke on his breath and clothing. "I'd like to speak with you about—"

"I think my homework instructions were clear enough."

"Yes, they were," Tasha replied, "but I wanted to talk to you about something else."

"Go on, then," the teacher said. "Hurry, though. This is my free period."

Tasha took a deep breath. "I want to take the county-wide math tests next weekend."

Mr. Cala raised a bushy eyebrow. "You mean next year, of course."

"No. I mean the next one coming up. I wanted to know if it's too late to enter."

"Not for a student who takes my math lessons seriously."

"I take your course seriously," Tasha insisted, though her brain was shouting, *It's you I don't take seriously.*

"You could have a good average if you applied yourself. But like most of you young ladies, your attention is more oriented toward your wardrobe than your future." His voice was almost a snarl.

"So can I take the test or what?"

"Miss Gordon," he said, shaking his head. "This math test is for serious students. They have studied hard, formed math teams and study groups. The scholarship award money will help those who want to further their math education, not their mall shopping allowance. I suggest you apply your energies to your classwork, where you are more likely to succeed ... perhaps."

"Are you saying no?" Tasha heard her voice rising.

"You can take the test, Miss Gordon," Mr. Cala said almost without moving his lips, "if you have the time to waste." With that, he was gone.

Tasha stood for some time trying to calm down and control her urge to suggest that Mr. Cala go for a swim in a lava pit. But it was no use, and as the second bell rang, she hurried off to gym class with the hope that basketball practice would help relieve some of her fury.

Tasha was in a special gym class that allowed the basketball team to practice together. The period was dedicated to tryouts for the team, and Tasha was looking forward to seeing what the new players would look like.

"We have six girls to try out in forty minutes," Mrs. Keiser, the coach, explained. "So everyone else please cooperate and take some seats on the bench."

Four of Tasha's teammates were in her class. Among them were Sheryl Johnson and Naomi Walker, two of the better players. The girls sat down next to Tasha, snickering as they reviewed the prospective members.

Six girls stood in their gym shorts and T-shirts awaiting instruction from the coach. Most of them were talking to one another, but Tasha noticed two who were busy limbering up. One was a tall, thin girl with short, curly hair. She didn't look very strong.

The other girl was of medium height, with reddish-brown hair. There was a cockiness to her appearance as she stared at the basket.

She's judging the height and distance, Tasha told herself. She may have something. But her teammates didn't share her views.

"Look at Ms. Attitude," Naomi said, pointing at the redhead. "She looks like we're wasting her time."

"Most of those girls look *too tired*," Sheryl said sarcastically. "I mean, look at that one over there."

Tasha followed her glance to a chunky girl with a short choppy hairdo. She looked very nervous, and her gym suit seemed a bit tight.

"She's got to stop letting her mommy dress her," Naomi added.

"Give them a chance." Tasha sighed. She knew team morale had been down a bit, but this was too much. "We didn't look like superstars when we first started."

Sheryl made a sucking sound through her teeth. "Well, we are now. And we need good players, as well as girls with style. I have an image to live up to."

Sheryl's and Naomi's remarks annoyed Tasha. They hadn't even seen what the other girls could do, and they were already making fun of them. Though it wasn't her whole life, Tasha loved playing basketball. She enjoyed the exercise, and the skill that went with the game. And she especially liked developing team strategy. Tasha knew the value of working together in the game, and she always remembered what her father had said. "You do your personal best, but you go out there as a team."

Her years of playing in sports had taught Tasha that players who thought they were the superstars usually weren't. She was beginning to wonder about Sheryl and Naomi.

For the next thirty minutes, Tasha and the others watched the tryouts. They saw fumbled passes, poor dribbling, and sloppy blocking. Three of the six girls had trouble hitting the backboard. And one seemed to get winded very easily.

All in all, it was not an encouraging session, and by the end, only two had showed any real potential. The redhead was one of them.

"Tasha and Naomi, please join us out here on the court." Mrs. Keiser stood with the two finalists, bouncing the ball impatiently.

Tasha had the feeling their coach wasn't any happier with the tryouts than they were.

"I want you two to go one-on-one with these two. Naomi, you take Sylvia," she said, pointing to an attractive girl with sharp features. "Tasha, it's you and Anna, here."

"Hi," Tasha said.

The redhead nodded but said nothing.

Naomi and Sylvia went first. Sylvia had trouble dribbling under Naomi's pressure and couldn't shoot from under the basket. But she scored five out of eight times shooting from the sides.

When it was over, Naomi gave her a nod of approval.

Tasha and Anna were up next. The coach tossed the ball into the air and both girls leaped to try and grab it. They weren't supposed to make contact, but when she grabbed the ball, Tasha felt Anna bump into her—hard. Mrs. Keiser shouted out a warning, but didn't stop them.

The girl was all over Tasha, pushing her just enough to throw her off but not enough for Tasha to know whether she meant to intimidate her.

When they were facing each other, Tasha could see a fierce determination in Anna's eyes. The girl could dribble well, and she had a nice way of protecting the ball with her body when she moved under the basket. Her short shots were good, but she hurried her outside shots and usually missed.

By the time Mrs. Keiser called "Game!" both girls were breathing hard, but Tasha had scored more points.

Anna Langley left the court when the mini-game was over, and didn't even stop to shake hands with Tasha.

"She's not that good," Sheryl said to Tasha. "And she's built like a tank."

"She's strong," Tasha said. "And she wants to win."

"So do the Boston Celtics," Naomi added. "Anyone have any hand lotion?"

Tasha rubbed her shoulder where Anna had bumped into her. "She's got a lot of...something," she said, half to herself. "I don't know if it's talent, though."

Mrs. Keiser announced the time of the next practice and called several of the new girls to one side.

"Maybe we should forget about these new players and find a star from another school who could transfer in," Naomi said. "These guys aren't going to get us anywhere."

Tasha noticed Mrs. Keiser speaking to Sylvia. "Maybe you're right," she told the others, as they entered the locker room. Then she noticed Anna staring at them. Had she heard? Tasha wondered. More than likely. The expression on Anna's face did not signal anything like friendship.

The redhead turned away, wrapped a towel around herself, and headed for the showers.

Competition seems to be the name of the game today, Tasha thought to herself. I came here hoping to cool out from Mr. Cala, but instead I ran into this girl. Lunch period has got to be better than this. She sighed and grabbed a facecloth.

Three

"It has nothing to do with her being white," Tasha told Sarah and Jennifer as she stood at their lunch table. Lunch period at Murphy High was one of the few times when Sarah and her friends could get together. All around them, the fifth-period kids gobbled down food, as they covered the latest gossip and gripes.

Tasha usually ate during sixth period, but she could often get out of study hall to meet the others for a few minutes. Today she had rushed to the lunchroom even faster than usual. Her session with Mr. Cala hadn't gone well, and it had certainly put her on edge. And the tryouts had left her feeling irritated with the world.

She'd hoped to find some sort of comfort and support from Sarah and her friends, but so far, even they seemed to be working against her.

"Anna Langley has already told five girls I know that the black girls on the basketball team were making fun of her," Jennifer remarked.

Tasha took a sip from her container of fruit juice. "They didn't mean anything by it. It was just talk."

"Sure," Sarah muttered.

"What's for lunch today?" April Winters asked as she joined the group.

"They call it chow mein," Kwame Brown replied. He dipped his fork into the stringy, greenish-brown substance on his plate. "But I'm betting the science department is missing a lab experiment gone bad."

"If it's anything but pizza or cinnamon buns, you give it a thumbs-down," April said, brushing back her long blond hair. "Kwame Brown, food critic to the stars!"

April was a sophomore at Murphy High, and new to the town of Madison. Until recently, her father's business had kept the family moving all over the country. Now they had finally settled down and April was truly happy to have friends like Sarah and Tasha, not to mention Cindy, Jennifer, and Kwame. It had finally made her life seem less like a fast-food menu.

"So if the team wasn't giving her a hard time because of her color, what was the problem?" Jennifer asked. She sniffled a bit and pulled a handkerchief from her bag.

22

"They thought she wasn't that good," Tasha replied. "It wasn't that big a deal."

"What color?" April asked.

"The way I heard it, the girls on the team were down on her the moment she arrived," Sarah said.

Tasha leaned forward over the table. "If she didn't make the team, she didn't make the team," she said. "It was her playing, and not her race. Anyway, we don't decide who's going to be on the team; the coach does."

"Is this a black thing?" April asked hesitantly.

Sarah laughed at her friend. "I don't think so, April, but it has nothing to do with you."

"We have Joan Gibbons on the team. She's white and no one is giving her a hard time," Tasha protested. "And how come you're fighting Anna's battles, anyway?"

"I'm just curious," Sarah said. "I'm not fighting anyone's battles."

Tasha let out a deep sigh and slipped into a seat next to Kwame. "Look, I didn't come here to debate the team ethics with you," she told Sarah. "I really came to ask Kwame if he's taking the math test."

"Not this time," Kwame answered as he bit into an egg roll. "Between my work on the school paper and the upcoming science exams, I'm straining my brilliance as it is."

"I thought I heard something squeaking," April said.

"That's cold," Kwame replied.

"Don't say cold around me," Jennifer complained as she dabbed her nose. "I think I'm coming down with a winner."

"Yeah," Kwame said. "You sound like you could star in one of those cold commercials."

"Tasha, you're really planning to enter the math contest?" Sarah asked.

"Absolutely," Tasha said. "There's no reason I can't represent the Gordon family. I might even walk away with a scholarship."

"Why'd you want to know if I was entering the contest?" Kwame asked. "Checking out the competition?"

"Not really," Tasha replied. "Because I'm entering so late, I need to learn as much about the test as possible."

"Didn't Mr. Cala give you the lowdown?" Jennifer asked.

"No, he did *not*," Tasha replied. She gave a brief account of her meeting with the math teacher. "All I got out of him was the clear impression that I'm not on his most favorite list."

"Well, I can't tell much, but I know who can." Kwame pointed to a tall boy sitting nearby with a number of other Asian students. "That's Brian Wu. He has to be taking the test."

"What makes you think so?" Sarah asked.

"That boy is math-mad," Kwame replied. "He can square pis and root quadratics with the best of them."

"Brian ran the lights for the Romeo Rap," Sarah reminded everyone.

"I remember him," April said. "He was lots of fun."

Kwame rose from the table. "Come on. I'll introduce

you to him. Brian and I are buddies from computer class."

Tasha nodded and the two of them strolled over to Brian's table.

To Tasha, Brian's thin, gold-rimmed glasses, shoulder-length black hair, and hawk-like features seemed both severe and friendly. He was busy telling a story with broad, animated movements as she and Kwame approached.

"Brian Wu, this is Tasha Gordon," Kwame said. "She's Sarah's cousin. They wrote the—"

"The Romeo Rap production I ran lights for," Brian said in a friendly way. He smiled at Tasha and introduced the other kids at the table. "Do you guys want to join us?"

"Just for a minute," Tasha said nervously.

"Tasha just decided to take the county-wide math test," Kwame explained. "She thought you might be able to clue her in on the game plan."

Tasha noticed several of the kids at the table eyeing her suspiciously. It suddenly occurred to her that she didn't know any of them. I bet Sarah does, she thought to herself.

"Why do you think Brian would have the answers?" said the girl Brian had introduced as Mae Ling Hu. She was attractive, with dark eyes that seemed to bore into Tasha as she spoke.

"I'm asking," Tasha replied evenly. "Who knows, I might get lucky."

Brian slipped an arm around Mae Ling and squeezed

25

gently. "No problem," he said. "I'll tell you what I can. Any friend of Kwame's and all that. But didn't the math department give you the lowdown?"

Tasha rolled her eyes. "Mr. Cala was less than cooperative."

"I know what you mean," Brian said, chuckling. "He's not one of my favorites, either. But he knows his stuff."

"He always takes the fun out of the classes," Tasha said.

"Not everyone is in school for a good time," Mae Ling said sarcastically.

Again Brian tried to calm her with a hug. "I think Mr. Cala had bigger ambitions for his life than teaching math," he told Tasha. "Did you ever notice he reads a lot of financial publications? Maybe he wanted to be a big Wall Street broker."

"I believe you're on to something there," Tasha said, smiling.

Mae Ling made a point of turning away from Tasha and started up a conversation with one of the others.

Brian chose to ignore her. "So," he said pleasantly, "what can I tell you about the math contest?"

"How is it set up?" Tasha asked.

Brian smiled. "There are two parts to it," he said. "The morning test is just regular stuff, regular but hard. You have thirty-five problems to deal with and not enough time. Then in the afternoon, if your brain hasn't turned to lasagna, you only have to do three problems out of ten. But they're killer problems. You have an hour and a half to do them."

"An hour and a half!" Tasha was stunned.

"That's if you don't go to the bathroom," Brian teased her. "Usually the judges grade the papers right after the test, and you know your score before you leave. But I hear they may do it differently this year."

"Oh, great." Tasha sighed and looked at Kwame, who simply shrugged.

"I heard that three years ago a guy took the test and his brain overheated and dripped out of his ears," Brian continued, "but if you do OK, I understand that a lot of schools will consider it when you're making out your college apps."

"Still interested?" Mae Ling asked.

Tasha ran her fingers through her hair. "Sure. Sounds like a barrel. Thanks for the help, Brian."

Tasha and Kwame said their good-byes and headed back to Sarah's table.

"What was the deal with her?" Tasha asked.

"I think she thought you were making moves on Brian," Kwame answered.

Tasha wrinkled her brow. "Why would I do that?"

"You're pretty, she's pretty. Isn't that reason enough?"

"Maybe," Tasha replied. "You were real quiet back there."

Kwame looked down at the floor. "Didn't have anything to say."

Tasha stopped walking. She'd forgotten how painfully shy Kwame could be when he wasn't with her and the gang. "Mae Ling wasn't the only pretty girl there. *You* could have made some moves."

"I'm saving up my fuel for the right ride," Kwame said. He busied himself wiping a tiny spot from his glasses.

"You're never going to find the girl of your dreams if you don't get out there, lover." Tasha smiled and gave him a small hug.

"I don't know," he replied. "I'm doing all right."

Kwame hadn't been looking at Tasha, but she knew what he meant. She knew he'd had a crush on her ever since she'd come to Murphy. At first she had encouraged it to rattle her cousin. It seemed Sarah had everyone following her around, listening to her every word.

But as she'd grown to know Sarah and her friends, Tasha had changed her mind. She'd begun thinking of Kwame as a friend—a very good friend. Maybe she'd also chosen not to notice that he might want something more. "I thought you were pining away for my cousin," she said as they continued walking.

"A man's entitled to check out the field," Kwame said.

"Just make sure the man isn't left standing out in the field," Tasha warned.

Kwame nodded but didn't say a word until he reached their table. Then his eyes lit up. "Hey, hey, Billy boy!" he said, greeting a new arrival. "How goes it, Guru?"

Tasha was surprised to see Billy Turner standing at the table. Billy was a friend of Dave Hunter's. They

28

both played on the school basketball team, and Billy had made more than his share of winning shots. And with his tight, lean frame, thin mustache, and short, razor-cut hairdo, Billy was definitely a popular man about town.

But Tasha knew Billy had a few strikes against him. For one, Sarah didn't like him at all. They had gone out on a couple of dates when Billy had suddenly introduced her to his *real* girlfriend. He claimed it had been a misunderstanding, but Sarah didn't want to hear it.

Since then, anything Sarah said about Billy was unprintable.

Tasha could tell by the look on Sarah's face that her feeling toward him hadn't changed.

"There you are, Kwame, my man!" Billy said as Tasha and Kwame joined the group. "I was just asking about you. Mr. Tanner wants us to drop by the Center today. He wants a report on the kids."

"No problem, Guru," Kwame replied.

"What's this Guru thing?" Tasha asked.

"What else do you call an A-number-one teacher?"

"Billy's a teacher?" April asked.

"It's no big deal," Billy said quickly.

Tasha thought he looked genuinely embarrassed. "What's no big deal?" she asked.

"Billy tutors some junior-high kids over at the Madison Community Center," Kwame explained. "These are kids that need extra help studying or grasping a particular subject for school."

"Some of them are kids with special problems, like

truancy, or language barriers—stuff like that," Billy said.

"How long have you been doing that?" Sarah asked skeptically.

"A couple of months now," Billy said. "The Center is near my house. I used to go there to play ball and stuff. When Mr. Tanner became the new director, he brought in all these new programs to help the kids in school. A lot of us were asked to help out—so I did."

"That sounds great," Jennifer said, fighting off a sneeze.

"Would you want to help out?" Billy asked quickly.

"Not me," Jennifer replied. "I am definitely not an A-plus student. The last thing some kid needs is me giving him wrong answers...unless you need fashion tips."

Billy chuckled. "I'll keep that in mind."

"Tell us some more about the program," Tasha asked as she sat down.

"Gladly." Billy smiled at her as he grabbed a chair.

As Billy talked, Tasha found that she liked the sound of his voice. She also liked the way he looked—lean, but powerful, with a strong chin and high cheekbones. Billy wore stylish but casual clothes, and a small gold earring in his left earlobe.

When Sarah had had her fling with Billy, Tasha had still been getting settled into her new home. She hardly remembered meeting him then. She wondered why she hadn't taken the time to really notice him before, then decided it didn't matter—she was noticing him now.

Moreover, Sarah noticed that she was noticing him. This could be fun, Tasha thought. She leaned back in her chair and crossed her legs. Her emerald-green spandex pants caught the light from the window and seemed to radiate.

It had the effect she wanted. Billy looked and smiled. "Contact," Tasha murmured.

"The tutoring program is really great," Kwame said, interrupting Billy's story. "I've only been there a short time, but I'd bet the rest of you could really get into it."

"Why don't we check it out?" Tasha asked Sarah. She could see her cousin wasn't comfortable with the thought of being involved with Billy again. "Look, we're always talking about doing things for the community, right?"

"Well, I —"

"And the Food for the Homeless fund-raiser was a success, right? After the Rap, we raised a lot of money."

"Yes, we did, but—"

"Then let's at least look into this." Tasha turned her attention to Billy. "I know I have some free time."

"Come on, Sarah," Kwame urged. "It can't hurt to check it out."

"Go on, girl," Jennifer said. Her voice sounded raspy and muffled. "What have you got to lose?"

"You sound worse," Tasha said.

"I feel worse." Jennifer sneezed into her handkerchief. "Suddenly pajamas and a cozy bed sound very appealing to me."

31

Kwame raised an eyebrow and leaned closer to Jennifer. "Same here."

Jennifer sneezed again, then smiled at Kwame. "Kiss me, you fool."

He suddenly leaned back. "After I get shots."

"Okay," Sarah said finally. "I'll go check this out."

"Great," Billy said. "You can come with Kwame and me this afternoon if you want."

"I'd love it," Tasha said evenly. Billy smiled at her. "I definitely would love it."

Four

The Madison Community Center was a large, one-story structure, on the corner of Lancaster and Clay avenues, about fifteen blocks from 18 Pine. Six blocks north, Lancaster was part of Madison's more active and attractive shopping district. But here, Tasha noticed, the neighborhood was older.

The houses were mostly rows of two- and three-story apartment buildings. It wasn't a run-down neighborhood, but there was a drabness to the buildings. Madison's town council hasn't extended its beautification program this far south, Tasha thought as she and the gang opened the steel-mesh doors.

"We sure don't have to work on their voice projection," Sarah called out to Cindy.

To say the place was noisy was an understatement. At first the girls had to put their hands over their ears to drown out the shouting and laughter echoing through the hallways.

"You'll get used to that," Kwame told Sarah. He had to raise his voice to be heard. "Maybe even before you lose your hearing."

Billy introduced everyone to a man sitting at a desk near the doors. The tag on his light blue shirt read "Security."

"My friends are here to check out the tutoring program, Lucas," Billy explained. "I'm trying to get them to volunteer for it."

"No problem, my man," Lucas replied. "Just sign in, then take 'em to see Mr. Tanner." Lucas gave a friendly nod to Kwame as he shoved a clipboard across the table. "Your session with little Josh didn't turn you off?"

"No way, my brother," Kwame said. "Once I convinced him that a conversation meant *both* people get to talk, we were fine."

Sarah looked stunned. "Excuse me?"

"No big deal," Kwame said with a shrug. "The kid I tutor thinks he has all the answers. His grades say otherwise. But he's smart, and he catches on fast. I've got hopes for him."

Tasha, Sarah, and Cindy had to sign a visitors' sheet before they were allowed to move through the

Community Center.

"Why all the high security?" Tasha asked.

Billy stopped in front of a gymnasium. Through the small glass windows, the girls could see a group of younger teens involved in a wild game of basketball.

"Things have gotten pretty heavy around here in the past two years," Billy explained. Tasha noticed that his easygoing manner had changed. He frowned as he gazed around the hallway. "The Center doesn't have the kind of problems you might find in the big city, but there have been thefts and even some gang troubles here."

"Not to mention some serious jerks who think joining in a study program is for wimps," Kwame added. "They sometimes hassle the kids coming or going."

Sarah and Cindy had moved farther down the corridor and were peeking through the windows in several closed doors.

"Find anything interesting?" Tasha asked as she joined them.

"They look like small classrooms," Sarah said, pointing through one of the windows. A few desks and chairs were crammed into a tiny room, along with a large bookshelf. A girl about Sarah's age sat at a table with two younger girls. They appeared to be studying a history book.

"That's Valenzia," Billy said. "She's been doing this for about a year, now—with the same two girls." He smiled. "She brought up their reading levels first—after that, there was no stopping them."

Tasha found herself staring at Billy. More and more she was feeling attracted to him, despite what Sarah had said. And when he spoke of the Center and the kids, Tasha could tell that he really cared. There was definitely more to Billy Turner than she had thought, and she was beginning to get the urge to check it out.

"Come on," Billy was saying as he led them farther down the corridor. "I'll take you to the office, where you can meet the main man."

"Mr. Tanner?" Cindy asked.

"Mr. Lawrence W. Tanner," Billy said with emphasis. "He's got the drive of an NBA lead player, but he looks like that singer...Sting."

"You mean he's British?" Sarah asked.

"Hardly. But he's real lean, has a thin pointy nose and scraggly blond hair."

"Scraggly?" came a stern voice from behind them.

The gang turned to see the man Billy had just described standing in the door of the room they had passed.

"You're in it now, brother," Kwame muttered to Billy.

"No offense, Mr. T.," Billy said quickly.

"That's debatable." Mr. Tanner moved toward the group with quick, easy strides.

Tasha couldn't tell how old he was, but it appeared that he dedicated all his energy to the Center. His clothes were shabby. His sweatshirt had the name of the Center printed across the front in plain black letters. In one hand he carried a loose-leaf notebook stuffed with papers. In the other was a half-eaten peanut butter and jelly sandwich.

"These are some of my friends from school," Billy said.

"Remarkable," Mr. Tanner said, eyeing the group. "And you all admit in public to being his friends?"

For a moment the gang couldn't tell if he was serious. Then a thin smile crept across his face.

"Actually, they're my friends, Mr. T.," Kwame said, throwing his arms around Tasha and Sarah.

"I find that almost as hard to believe," Mr. Tanner replied without missing a beat. He took a bite from his sandwich as he started off down the hall. "I suspect you are here to see our tutoring program. Follow me and I'll show you our wonderful world of fertile but untilled minds. Perhaps you will decide to become farmers of knowledge."

"I think I'm going to like this place," Tasha told Sarah. Her cousin nodded in agreement.

Mr. Tanner led the group in and out of game rooms, small offices, and even a lounge area. In each place, older teens sat giving instructions, or guiding younger teens through some lesson plan. Speaking rapidly, Mr. Tanner explained how every inch of space had to be put to use.

"We don't have a great deal of county or state funding to support us," he explained, "so it's unlikely we'll see a larger facility anytime in the near future."

"So you make do with what you have," Sarah said sympathetically.

Mr. Tanner grunted. "And we do it very well." He led them out the back door to the Center's parking lot. Tasha spotted a large trailer off to the left. "This forty-foot monster was donated to us by a local contractor," Mr. Tanner said as they walked toward it.

"It looks like the type they use as offices at construction sites," Cindy said in amazement.

"They are also found," Mr. Tanner said as he opened the door, "in the playgrounds of overcrowded schools, where they serve as extra classroom space. And that's why it is here."

The inside looked much like the classroom they had seen inside the Center. A few small desks stood against one wall, and a portable chalkboard and two short bookcases stood near the other. Papers were scattered around the room as if a hurricane had whipped through the narrow space.

"We had some kids in here earlier," Mr. Tanner explained. He frowned. "They're working on math. Please sit."

Tasha, Sarah, and Cindy sat at the small desks. Kwame stood by Mr. Tanner, and Billy leaned against the wall very near Tasha.

"That's our happy little operation," Tanner said. "How does it look to you?"

"I'm impressed," Sarah said.

"Same here," Cindy agreed.

"If you have any desire to come on board, there are at least two students I can think of right away."

"My father is the principal at Hamilton High," Sarah

said. "So I know how important programs like these are to the community. You can count me in."

"How about you?" Billy asked Tasha.

Tasha was also impressed with the Center's program, and she was seriously considering donating some of her time. Especially since her wonder-woman cousin had already volunteered. And when she looked up into Billy's light brown eyes, she found another reason to join. "The facilities and the *staff* look good to me," she said. "I guess I can be persuaded to do my part."

"Excellent," said Mr. Tanner. He was already heading out the door. "I'll be back with the prospective victims in a minute."

"Well," Kwame said after the Center director had left. "Me and Billy have fresh young minds waiting to be twisted...uh, enlightened, by our dazzling Euro/Afrocentric wit, so..."

"We'll see you girls later?" Billy asked, not taking his eyes off Tasha.

"You'll see *one* of us later, I suspect." Sarah's voice dripped with sarcasm.

"Are you really interested in him?" Sarah asked after the boys had left. "After what he did?"

"Sarah, he tried to use you to get out of a relationship with another girl. It was stupid," Tasha said.

"That's for sure," Cindy said.

"He lied to me," Sarah insisted.

"Then he told you the truth and introduced you to the other woman. Seems to me that he wasn't up to lying for long. He came clean, and that means he's worth checking out. That . . . and the fact that he is definitely fine."

"That's for sure," Cindy repeated and smiled.

"Thanks for your support," Sarah told Cindy, then smiled in spite of herself. "Okay, I'll admit he's cute, concerned about the right things, and—last I heard—totally available."

"Don't worry, cousin. I promise I'll go easy on him."

Sarah simply shook her head. "It's your dream, girl."

A moment later, Mr. Tanner returned with two kids who looked to be about thirteen or fourteen years old.

"This is Melissa Lucarelli and Kenny Freeman," Mr. Tanner said as he ushered them into the room. "And these," he pointed to Tasha, Sarah, and Cindy, "are the new schoolmarms."

Melissa gave a faint nod to the girls. She was a fair-skinned girl with long, wavy black hair and dark eyes. She wore thick eye shadow and grayish-black lipstick. Tasha couldn't help thinking of Morticia in *The Addams Family.*

Kenny stood out in his own style. He wore a baggy denim outfit over a white hooded sweatshirt. The hood was pulled up over his head, covering a red baseball cap. He had a smile that made Tasha think of a shark eyeing a school of minnows.

Kenny took a seat on the corner of one of the desks. "If school looked this good, the teacher could get me to do anything."

He stared at Cindy, who gave him a get-real look.

"I'd be on time every time," Kenny told Tasha.

40

"To be on time," Tasha replied sweetly, "you have to know *what time it is*."

Melissa snickered and sat down next to Sarah.

Kenny eyed Tasha for a second, then smiled. "You don't understand me. See, I got my own program," he said, his hands moving with expression and energy. "I'm a hawk in the wind, a free-spirit man."

"Knowledge is freedom," Sarah said. "Don't think it isn't."

Kenny sneered. "Yeah, right. See, I'm smokin' on the court. B-ball's my thing. I'm gonna be a superstar doing commercials for sneakers and cruisin' in my own limo, making stupid big money! What do I need math and English for?"

Tasha rose from her chair and picked up her coat. "Maybe so you'll know how much you made and where you put it."

"Oooo, she got you there!" Melissa said.

Kenny looked irritated. "I'll have people to take care of that stuff."

"Maybe," Tasha said. "But how will you know if they cheat you?"

"What would you know about it?" Kenny said angrily.

"My father was a pro football player. I know all about it." She met Kenny's hard stare. "If you're nice, sometime I'll tell you about it."

"Melissa, are you into this program?" Sarah asked.

"Yeah, kinda." Melissa shrugged and looked out the window. "Teachers say I can't pick up on things."

"Is that true?" Sarah pressed.

"I don't know." Melissa thought for a moment. "No. I'm not stupid."

"My grandmother always says that's where it starts."

"What?"

"Learning," Sarah replied. "She says the day you know you can is the day you start. We'll find out."

"Do I take it that at least two of you want to come back?" Mr. Tanner asked nonchalantly.

Sarah looked at Cindy. "All of us do."

"Excellent," he said eagerly. "Fresh victims." He smiled as the girls headed out the door. "Honestly," he said when they were halfway across the parking lot, "thank you."

Tasha, Sarah, and Cindy said good-bye and headed home.

PINE

Five

When Tasha got home, she found Allison sitting in the living room. Her legs were folded under the coffee table and she was bent over her loose-leaf notebook, pen poised, eyes vacant. She had her portable tape player plugged into her ears. It was so loud Tasha could hear the music from across the room.

"Are you seriously into that tune?" she asked, pulling away one of the earphones. "Or are you trying to scramble what little brains you have?"

"Oh boy, that's original," Allison replied. "Where's Sarah? I want to ask her something."

"She walked Cindy home. I think they wanted to talk

about me." Tasha tried to run her fingers through Allison's hair, but it was too tangled. "You've been twisting your hair again."

Allison rolled her eyes. "I always do when I'm working on something that's really hard."

"What is it?" Tasha looked over Allison's shoulder at the notebook.

"I'm trying to figure out what a barn in a snowstorm has to do with anything," Allison said.

"Excuse me?"

"My English teacher is on this poetry kick," Allison explained. "She told us we could read any poetry we wanted to and then write about it and discuss it in class."

"So what did you choose?" Tasha pulled her Afropick from her purse, sat down and started combing out Allison's hair.

"Are you kidding?" Allison said. "The only poetry I'm into is rap. So me and some other kids brought in the lyrics to our favorite songs. But . . ."

"It didn't go over."

"No way. Now she's got us reading stuff by Robert Frost and this woman, Gwendolyn Brooks or something. I never heard of her."

"Never heard of Gwendolyn Brooks, the black poet? That's a riot." Tasha smiled. "I had to do the same thing," she confided. "You'll survive."

"Why can't we write about rap? That's a kind of poetry."

"Really?" Tasha asked.

"Sure," Allison said. "Look how it worked with Shakespeare, in Sarah's Romeo Rap thing. Everybody's still talking about that show."

There it is again, Tasha thought. Spotlight on Sarah Gordon. Polly Perfect wins again. "Well, we're all happy about that news, aren't we."

Allison could hear the sarcasm in Tasha's voice. "Who stepped on your toes?"

"No one," Tasha snapped.

"Sure," Allison said skeptically. "You need some help studying for the math test or something? Want me to ask you some questions?"

"No, thanks," Tasha replied. A wave of renewed anger washed over her as she thought about what Mr. Cala had said. "I'm fine. In fact, I'm so prepared that I'm going to give myself a treat tonight. A warm, luxurious bath, complete with scents, oils, and soft music." She grabbed up her things and headed up the stairs. "Call me when dinner is ready."

18 PINE

Six

Thursday held more than one surprise for Tasha. There was a line of students waiting outside the math department office when she went to sign up.

"All you guys here to sign up for the math test?" she asked.

"For sure," said the girl ahead of her.

"I didn't think math had such a following."

"No way," the girl replied, flinging her hair back and popping her gum. "But there's scholarship money here, if you know what I mean. A person would have to be totally dense not to go for it."

Tasha did know what she meant. Though her parents

had left her well provided for, a college scholarship would certainly come in handy. But she suddenly realized that winning it might be a little bit harder than she thought.

Soon a secretary came out and distributed applications to the kids in the line. As Tasha began filling in the information, Brian Wu walked out of the office.

"I thought you'd already signed up for this," she told him.

Brian brushed his bangs away from his eyes. "I did. They just needed some additional info. So, you're going to go for it, huh?"

"Sure," Tasha said coyly. "Afraid of a little competition?"

"Not even," he replied cheerfully. He looked at the others on the line and stepped closer to Tasha. "Half of these kids won't even show up for the afternoon part," he whispered.

"It's that hard?"

"That hard and that tricky," Brian answered. "Remember, this is a county-wide competition. Kids will be coming from all over, so the system has to cut down the odds early. My cousin took the test last year and said it was a real grind. When you figure out how to solve the problems, then you have to work them out, and that takes forever."

"They should let you use a calculator," Tasha said.

"But they don't." Brian shook his head. "It's part of their torture method to give you as many chances to blow it as possible."

Suddenly Tasha felt even less confident. "You said most of these kids. You don't include me in that group?"

"Not really. Kwame told me you were pretty smart." Brian's dark brown eyes sparkled. "He was right on both counts."

"Careful what you say," Tasha replied. "Your *friend* wouldn't like it."

Brian smiled pleasantly. "Mae Ling is a little sensitive about a great many things."

Tasha gave him a quizzical look. "Have you been straying?"

"Nothing like that. She and I are solid. She's just a little possessive."

"Tell me about it." Tasha made a clucking sound with her tongue.

"She's OK." Brian leaned up against the wall next to Tasha. "My first girlfriend, really..."

Tasha felt a little uncomfortable. She wondered if Brian was leaning so close to her on purpose. "Now that you've got the hang of it, are you ready for the big time?" she asked.

"What?" Brian's brow furrowed.

"Forget it," Tasha said. "Tell me, how did you wind up liking math so much?"

"Partly for myself, partly for family. My folks want me to have it better than they did. You know the rap."

Tasha nodded. She knew her grandparents had expected her father and uncle to do better than they had done. Even after her father had made it, he was always worrying about what his folks thought.

"My folks work crazy hours to put me and my older sisters through school," Brian was saying.

"Do they all go to college?" Tasha asked.

"Two did." Brian snickered. "One of them decided she wanted to be on her own. She's out there *somewhere...*" Brian let the word fade away, expressing how his sister had drifted out into the world.

"So you're next up," Tasha said.

"If the dollars are there," Brian replied nonchalantly.

"Next!" the math department secretary called.

Tasha realized it was her turn. "It's been nice talking to you," she told Brian as she grabbed her book bag. "See you at the test."

"Believe it." Brian gave her a peace sign and strolled off down the hallway.

Tasha entered the math department office, and as the secretary processed her registration, she couldn't help remembering something Mr. Cala had said. "Students who are serious about furthering their math education..."

Brian was serious. Was she? It bothered her that she didn't really know.

The second surprise of the day came as Tasha was on her way to her seventh-period class. She felt a hand gently take hold of her shoulder.

"How goes it?" Billy Turner asked as he fell into step alongside her.

Tasha smiled. "It's getting better." She liked the way

50

Billy looked. He wore a white, collarless shirt, buttoned at the neck, and a pair of tight black jeans.

"So where are you headed?" Billy asked.

"Room Three-twenty-two. Chemistry. Mr. Fabian is out today, so I'm not in any hurry."

"That's on my way. I'll walk you," Billy said.

"Where's your next class?" Tasha asked.

"One-oh-six. French."

Tasha had to laugh. "That's two floors down and on the other side of the building."

"Sometimes the best distance between where you are and where you want to be is the long way."

"How now, Mr. Smooth." Tasha smiled.

"You and Sarah set up your schedule at the Center yet?" Billy asked.

"We've talked to Mr. Tanner about it."

Billy seemed to think twice about asking his next question. "You and Sarah talk about me?"

"Intimately. Nervous?"

"Let's say, I know I made a mistake," Billy replied. "But I only want to pay for it once. What I did with Sarah was stupid."

"No argument," Tasha said.

"I apologized," Billy said quietly. "I'd like to put it away . . . if that's possible."

"Why are you telling me all of this?" Tasha asked.

"Because I'd like the chance to get to know you," Billy answered. "I thought maybe sometime we—"

"Sometime we can," Tasha interrupted. "Maybe even soon." Just then she spotted Kwame standing near the door to Room 322, apparently watching them closely.

"Here we are," she said as they reached the room. "Hey, Kwame."

"Yo Kwame," Billy said.

"What's happening?" Kwame responded. He kept shifting his gaze from Tasha to Billy.

"I'd better get inside," Tasha told Billy. "See you around?"

"Bet on it." Billy gave her a dazzling smile, gave Kwame a high five, and headed off down the corridor.

Tasha watched and admired his smooth, easy stride. She suspected he could be smooth in many other ways, too.

"I just wanted to ask if you signed up for the math contest," Kwame said, disturbing Tasha's train of thought.

"Signed, sealed, and ready for action."

Kwame watched Billy disappear at the far end of the corridor. "Yeah, you and Billy both."

Tasha studied Kwame's face. She wasn't certain, but she thought he looked upset. "I thought you and Billy were friends."

Kwame nervously adjusted his glasses. "We are."

"Then what's wrong?"

Kwame didn't answer right away. "Sarah doesn't like him very much."

Tasha sighed heavily. "Sarah and I are two different people, in case you hadn't noticed."

"I have. It's just that, well—" Kwame looked embarrassed. Just then a beeping noise started.

"What's that?" Tasha asked.

"It's my new pocket computer. My dad gave it to me for my birthday," Kwame answered. "It's got an alarm, memory, and sixteen levels of hierarchical calculating power."

"I've got to get inside," Tasha told him. "Where you headed?"

"The computer room, just down the hall. Same place I always go seventh period . . . after I say hi to you." Kwame started off down the hall. "I guess you just forgot."

"Hey, how good are those hand-held computers?" Tasha asked.

"Some are great," Kwame answered, walking backward down the hall. "Some of the ones they have now are more powerful than the ones they used when they built the atom bomb."

"Did I hear Kwame say you were building an atomic bomb?" Cindy dropped her books on Tasha's desk.

"He was talking about computers," Tasha said. "Where did you get those earrings?"

"A cousin sent them all the way from St. Kitts," Cindy said, taking off one of the earrings so that Tasha could take a closer look. It was a real feather, almost pure white with brown markings, and mounted in a gold setting.

"Super fine," Tasha said.

The math test came to mind as she handed the delicate earring back to her friend and remembered what

Mr. Cala had said about not being serious. *Hey,* came a small voice from deep within her, *it's all right to like earrings and math, too.*

that you could harm the reputation of the school?"

"What is the problem?" Tasha asked. "I'm going to give it a shot. It's no big deal."

"Without proper preparation, you haven't got a chance of doing well tomorrow." Mr. Cala appeared to be sneering at her. "That's the big deal."

Tasha held back the words she really wanted to say. "Well, excuse me for living, Mr. Cala."

"It's a shame you young women never choose to meet a challenge properly."

Tasha shook her head as if her teacher's words were some annoying bug droning in her ear. "Excuse me, Mr. Cala," she said. "Just what do you mean, *you young women never—*"

"Fathers train their sons to meet challenges force-fully," Mr. Cala said without hesitation. "They do this through playing football, wrestling, and other contact sports. Boys carry this training into their academic studies. They aggressively attack math the way they would any other opponent. It's not your fault. It is a matter of your upbringing."

Tasha felt her shoulders tighten.

"Girls are more tentative in sports," the teacher went on, "and more passive in other areas. They shy away from approaching the bigger problems."

"Mr. Cala," Tasha replied, trying to remain calm, "I'm meeting this challenge the way my *father* taught me to meet anything, head-on."

"We'll see," Mr. Cala said sarcastically.

Murphy High must have a time machine, Tasha

thought as she walked to her seat. That's the only way they could have hired a genuine Neanderthal.

She was so angry she couldn't think straight for the rest of math class. It wasn't just being angry at Mr. Cala, though. She was also wondering if he was right, which made her even angrier. She kicked her desk and held back the urge to scream.

Fifth-period lunch was noisy. Moreso when Mr. Kenner made his announcement. "This is just a friendly and timely reminder to all students who are participating in tomorrow's math contest." The principal's voice crackled over the lunchroom loudspeaker. "Just remember, hard work and concentration will add up to success. Good luck and remember, starting time is nine o'clock *sharp*."

"Mr. Kenner loves to use the PA system," Holly Chambers told Tasha. Holly was a short, curly-haired blond girl who was in Tasha's French class. "I mean, he's okay and all. But boy, is he gung-ho."

Tasha agreed with Holly. Like most of the kids, she joked about Mr. Kenner's eager attitude and his attempts to be "down" with the kids, but she actually liked him. She knew he really cared about his students, just like her Uncle Donald.

"Is anything wrong?" Holly asked. "You've been pretty quiet most of the period."

"I'm all right," Tasha said. She gazed around the crowded, noisy cafeteria. "I'm just bothered by something Mr. Cala said."

58

"Is he still bugging you about the test?"

"Yeah."

"Later for him," Holly shot back. "He did the same thing to me."

"You're taking the math test?" Tasha asked, trying to conceal her surprise.

"No, but he failed me in math last semester just because I had a low average."

"Holly, what was your average?"

"With or without dividing?" Holly asked. She had a grin on her face.

"With or without dividing what?" Tasha asked.

"Well, if you add up my four test scores, you get one hundred and forty." Holly twirled a lock of hair around one finger. "Which is really good."

"But if you divide it to get an average..." Tasha said.

"He divided," Holly said. "I thought he was going to." They both started laughing.

Billy Turner eased into a chair next to her. "Hey, hey, Holly."

"Hi, Billy." Holly picked up on the looks between Tasha and Billy and grinned knowingly. "Well, I've got things to do, so you two will excuse me? See you later," she told Tasha.

Billy turned and watched as Holly walked away.

"I thought you ate during fourth period," Tasha said, watching Billy turn back to look at her.

"No, I was just there the other day to get Kwame." His gaze shifted to the opened math books next to her.

"You trying to memorize that stuff?"

"Trying."

"Maybe you should light some candles or something," Billy said.

Tasha raised an eyebrow. "Excuse me?"

"I just meant, with you coming on late and being up against kids like Brian Wu, Tony Alberte, and Marty Shaw, well you know, I mean—"

"Pretend I don't," Tasha said dryly.

"Yo, look, those dudes are into some heavy math. I wouldn't be surprised if one of them became a rocket scientist or something."

"And women?"

"I'm not saying that women can't be good at math." Billy grinned. "You've got to handle recipes and stuff like that."

Tasha's eyes flashed with anger as she raised her plate. "And how about me calculating how hard a tuna sandwich can impact against somebody's head?"

"Whoa! Whoa!" Billy yelled, holding up his hands. "I was just kidding, honest! My mother is good at math."

Tasha stared at him for a long moment before she finally lowered the plate. "Is she really?"

"She sure is," Billy replied anxiously. "She's a stock analyst in the city. Has been for years."

"I didn't know that," Tasha said.

Billy gave a sigh of relief. "There's a lot you don't know about me, Tasha. So how about giving us both a chance to learn?"

"When?" she asked.

"Tonight."

Tasha hesitated. She really hadn't studied very much, and Mr. Cala had said the test began exactly at nine.

"Come on, Tasha," Billy pleaded. "If you're worried about tomorrow, we can make it an early evening. I'll have you in by twelve." Tasha began to object, but Billy cut her off. "Okay, okay, eleven o'clock." He moved a little closer to her.

Tasha caught the scent of sandalwood cologne on his skin. These were the wild times, she told herself.

"Please," Billy said softly.

"I guess I can always study in the morning," she said finally. "Okay, pick me up at seven tonight."

"Bet," Billy answered enthusiastically.

I need to relax, Tasha told herself as they sat and talked. Her father had always joked that an uptight player made mistakes.

She suddenly realized she was remembering a lot of things her parents had said. Why? In a few days it would be the anniversary of their deaths. Tasha felt a sudden chill run through her. She began wringing her hands together under the table, hoping Billy wouldn't notice.

"You're going out tonight?" Sarah stood in the center of Tasha's room, helping her cousin slip into a short, form-fitting red dress. Even in the dull room light, the satin-like material gleamed.

"Billy's taking me to SWEATS. It's a—"

"It's that teen club across town." Sarah sighed. "I have a life, too."

"Okay," Tasha said. "Then you know they don't sell alcohol, so Billy and I will be safe and sober." She slipped on black pumps. "And you heard me tell Aunt Elizabeth, I'll be home by eleven or so. I promise."

"Don't promise me anything," Sarah said. She was genuinely concerned. "You're the one with the monumental test tomorrow."

"You're right," Tasha replied. "Look, would you help me cram in the morning?"

Sarah placed her hands on her hips. "Sure, wreck my beauty sleep for your own selfish purposes."

"Cousin," Tasha said as she grabbed Sarah's hands. "I really need this night out."

"All right," Sarah said as her shoulders sagged. "I'll help, but—"

"Thanks!"

The doorbell rang and Tasha heard Allison racing to the door. "My date is here," she said, throwing on a long black coat. "And I don't want Allie to ask any dumb questions."

"Tell Billy if he steps out of line, he'll be the target of half the girls at Murphy," Sarah told Tasha.

A quick hug and Tasha was gone.

Eight

Mrs. Gordon was standing by the front door talking to Billy when Tasha came downstairs. As she expected, Allison was right there, bombarding Billy with questions.

"I thought you were interested in my sister Sarah," she said.

"Sarah and I are just friends," Billy answered awkwardly.

"But you took her on two—"

"It is Billy and Tasha who are going out this evening," Mrs. Gordon said, interrupting her younger daughter. "And I believe your sister's business should remain her business. I'm certain Mr. Turner wouldn't think of placing anyone in this house in a compromising position." Mrs. Gordon raised an eyebrow. "Would you, Mr. Turner?"

Tasha saw Billy swallow hard before he answered. "No, ma'am. That would certainly be the farthest thing from my mind."

Mrs. Gordon noticed Tasha approaching. "Right answer."

"I'll be home soon," Tasha told her aunt as they kissed good-bye.

"Have fun," Mrs. Gordon said.

As they walked to Billy's car parked at the curb, Tasha could feel her aunt watching them from the porch.

"It doesn't look like much," Billy said, indicating the car as he slid behind the wheel. "But it goes the distance in almost any weather."

"It looks fine to me," Tasha said pleasantly.

Billy took a moment to gaze at Tasha and her outfit. "Same here," he said. "You look just great."

"Thanks. And so do you," Tasha replied. Billy was wearing a brown collarless leather jacket, tan pants, and a white turtleneck. "Now let's go somewhere," Tasha said with a smile, "and let the world get an eyeful."

SWEATS was an assault on the senses. Tasha could feel its pulse the moment they stepped from the car.

The club was in a large one-story building on the

outskirts of town. The stucco exterior was painted white, and a black canvas awning extended out to a circular driveway. On top of the roof, a hot-pink, yellow, and tropical-green neon sign flashed the name SWEATS. It could be seen for blocks in any direction.

Inside was one huge room, done in high-tech style, with strobes, spots, and tracer lights splashing colors everywhere. The bar served fancy nonalcoholic drinks, and the food was mostly burgers and appetizers. The place was jumping.

Kids were dressed to kill, dancing to music coming through a state-of-the-art sound system.

Tasha began dancing the moment they had checked their coats. "We don't have a lot of time," she shouted over the music. "So let's set the roof to burn!"

"I hear you," Billy shouted back as he followed her out onto the crowded floor.

Tasha whirled and rocked with the rhythm. Her hair whipped wildly about.

When a slow song played, she eased into his strong, gentle embrace. The scent of his cologne surrounded her along with the lights and the music.

This is perfect, she told herself. It's just what I need.

At the end of the evening, as she kissed Billy good-night on the front porch, Tasha felt that perfection again. "Can I see you tomorrow?" Billy whispered. "After the test?"

"Count on it," Tasha replied softly. They kissed again, and then Billy said good-night and went home.

When Tasha went to bed, the music was still playing in her head, and she could still feel his lips on hers.

"Perfect," she whispered. "Absolutely perfect."

"What postulate of Euclidean geometry is discarded in non-Euclidean geometry?" Sarah stared across the top of her cousin's geometry book. Tasha's face looked pinched. The normal brightness of her eyes was dulled.

She looked tired and worried. "Am I supposed to know that at seven o'clock in the morning?" she moaned.

"Yes. And you're supposed to know it at nine o'clock A.M. when you sit down to take the test."

Tasha sat up on her bed and ran her fingers through her hair. "Maybe I'll get it after I shower."

"No good, party girl," Sarah teased. But there was an element of concern in her voice. "If you want that shower, you'd better come up with the answer."

"Postulate ... Euclidean geometry ..." Tasha muttered. "It's something to do with—lines!" she exclaimed. "The answer is the parallel postulate!"

"Right!" Sarah cheered.

"Now may I have that shower?" Tasha asked sleepily.

"Naturally," Sarah said slyly as she followed Tasha into the bathroom, book in hand. "But if you want soap you'll have to tell me how to do logarithms."

Tasha sent a towel flying at her cousin.

At 9:00 A.M. Tasha sat in a classroom at Hamilton High School.

It was strange to be there in the first place. She'd never really had a reason for visiting the school before. The fact that her uncle was the principal at Hamilton made it feel even stranger.

Hamilton wasn't too much different from her own high school. It appeared to be as ancient as Murphy, with its old-fashioned stone and brick design. But several of its outer walls were covered with graffiti, and wire-mesh grills covered most of the first-floor windows.

There was no large lawn. Hamilton spanned half a city block, with only a few trees and bushes running along its walls.

Inside, the halls were well kept, but they seemed less festive than Murphy's. The walls and columns were painted hospital green and maroon, rather than bright primary colors.

Tasha remembered hearing her uncle comment that he wanted to brighten up the school's environment, to help his students want to learn. But the school board couldn't see the connection. Tasha certainly could. She was glad she went to Murphy.

There were twenty others in the room with Tasha, one in every other seat. Brian Wu was in the next room with another group.

"Remember," said Mr. Olsen, the proctor, "you can get partial credit on problems and you're not penalized for wrong answers. Is that understood?"

A few of the kids nodded. Tasha noticed that there were only two other girls in the room.

"If you have any questions, raise your hand and ask me," Mr. Olsen said. He was about fifty, Tasha thought, and sort of nice-looking for an older man. Distinguished. "You'll get your results on Tuesday. And I know I don't have to tell you to keep your eyes on your own papers."

When the signal was given Tasha opened the printed test booklet and read the first question. An image of Mr. Cala flashed through her mind.

The first question looked impossible. So did the second. The third looked possible and she started working on it.

The first hour was hard, and the second hour was harder. Tasha felt sick, she felt hot, she felt cold—everything but good. The room was quiet except for the scratching of pencils on paper.

Tasha wasn't sure about anything. In fact, even things she knew were beginning to look strange. She needed a break. She took a deep breath and raised her hand.

Mr. Olsen came over and Tasha told him that she had to go to the bathroom. He took her to the door and then called over another teacher, also male, and whispered something in his ear.

"There's no monitor for the girls," the other teacher said.

"Is this bathroom visit, uh, absolutely necessary?" Mr. Olsen asked Tasha.

"Yes. I gotta go." Tasha said with a smile.

The second teacher took Tasha to the girls' bathroom

and stood outside the door.

Inside the bathroom Tasha splashed her face with cold water. It made her feel better. From the bathroom window she could see kids playing a pickup basketball game in the schoolyard. She ran some more cold water onto a paper towel and put the cold towel on the back of her neck. It felt good, really good.

The rest of the morning test went well enough. She was still stumped by the first question, and ended up guessing at it.

After the first test ended, the hallway was filled with groans.

"Are they kidding me?" a short boy Tasha recognized from 18 Pine asked. "You gotta have two brains to get those questions. Maybe three brains."

"It wasn't so bad," another boy said. "I just wish the test wasn't given in Greek."

"Greek?" Tasha looked at him.

"Well," the boy said, with a wide grin, "it was Greek to me."

Brian came over and asked Tasha how she had done. She shrugged. "It was hard," she said.

"Right," he said. "And that was the easy part."

In the afternoon there were only fifteen kids in her room. Five must have dropped out of the test, Tasha thought.

Brian was right. The afternoon questions were killers. She only had to answer three, but each question had three parts to it. They were hard, but they were also interesting, and she tackled them with a plan. She would do two, then take a bathroom break as she had in the morning, then do the last one.

It took a full hour to finish the two problems she had selected, and she thought about skipping the break. But when she didn't see another question in the set that she thought she could solve easily, she raised her hand.

"Again?" Mr. Olsen asked.

Tasha nodded.

Even as she went through the ritual of washing her face in cold water she was thinking about the other questions. She thought she had a clue on one of them, and by the time she got back to her seat she was pretty sure of it. She finished it and was about to start checking her answers when she heard Mr. Olsen's voice. "Time!" he called. "Pencils down!"

At 3:15, Tasha walked out of Hamilton High like a zombie. She stared across the street, to the park, and wished she were somewhere else, anywhere.

"How'd it go?" Billy Turner asked, stepping out of his car.

"Can we go for a walk in that park?"

"Sure. The car's okay here."

They strolled across the grass and stopped by a small pond. Billy leaned against an old cedar.

"I tried," Tasha said after a moment. "I didn't answer all the questions. They were so hard."

Billy looked genuinely concerned as he put an arm around her. "Do you think you passed?"

"It's not a pass/fail test. If it were, I guess I would have passed. But compared to all the other people in

70

there, I don't know," Tasha replied.

"When will you know?"

"We'll get our results on Tuesday."

Three days. Tasha wasn't sure she could stand the wait.

PINE

Nine

As dusk settled in on the Gordon house, the smell of burgers and hot dogs mingled with the aroma of charcoal and toasted buns.

Mr. Gordon stood in the backyard, merrily singing, spatula in one hand and barbecue sauce in the other.

"How'd you get Uncle Donald to cook out on a cold night like this?" Tasha asked her aunt.

"It's his way of making up for Miss Essie's stew the other night," Mrs. Gordon replied. "Besides, it's the only safe way to put fire, food, and my husband together." She opened the back door for Allison, who was carrying in a plate of barbecued corn.

"How can Dad stand out there like that?" Allison shivered as she set the plate on the table. "All he has on is a couple of sweaters."

"The heat of the fire is one reason," Tasha told her.

"And?" Allison asked.

Mrs. Gordon and Tasha exchanged amused glances. "It's a man thing," they said in unison and laughed.

Allison looked confused.

Mrs. Gordon chuckled. "Of course your grandmother happened to choose tonight to eat out with friends."

"Where's Sarah?" Tasha asked.

"She and Cindy went to the movies," Allison replied.

"Will she be back in time to eat with us?" Tasha asked.

"Believe it," Allison declared. "As soon as she smells barbecued burgers, she'll head home like a rocket."

Fifteen minutes later, Sarah came through the door, and everyone sat down to eat.

"I still say we should have eaten outside on the deck tables," Mr. Gordon said.

"It's nearly dark as pitch out there and at least thirty-five degrees," Mrs. Gordon said.

"More like forty, I'd say," Mr. Gordon replied.

"Whatever."

"It's warmer in here, Dad," Sarah added. "And the food's just as good."

Tasha had to agree that the corn was juicy and sweet, the burgers were cooked just right, and the sauce was hot and spicy. "I love this sauce," she told her uncle. "What brand is it?"

Mr. Gordon raised an eyebrow. "Brand?"

"Uh-oh," Allison said in mock fear. "Here comes the legend."

"I'll have you know that this sauce is an old Gordon family recipe, handed down from father to son for five generations."

"Why did only the men get the recipe?" Tasha asked.

"The women were too smart to take it," Mrs. Gordon teased.

Mr. Gordon pretended to snarl at her. "My father took many hours to teach me how to prepare this. The tomatoes, the seasonings. The long days of waiting while the special ingredients—"

"Many of them too complex even for a Nobel prize-winning scientist," Tasha said.

"Waiting while the ingredients blend," her uncle continued. He slowly looked over everyone at the table. "Perhaps I will pass it on to one of you, should you prove worthy."

Allison frowned. "I don't think so. Cooking doesn't fit into my future. No way."

"And just how do you plan to eat?" Mrs. Gordon asked.

"I'll eat out, or order in," Allison declared.

Mr. Gordon chuckled as he turned to Tasha. "Your father never told you about this age-old family ritual?"

Tasha shrugged. "I guess it was just one more thing he didn't have time for." As she bit into her burger, she wondered why she had said that. It wasn't a big deal.

"We've been meaning to ask you, Tasha." Mrs. Gordon spoke carefully. "What do you want to do on Wednesday?"

"Go to school, eat pizza, and celebrate my math results."

"How was the test?" Sarah asked.

Again Tasha felt tense and uncomfortable. "I don't know, actually. It was hard, but I might have done OK. It's hard to tell because the questions were really tricky."

"But you did answer them?" Mr. Gordon raised one eyebrow.

"Best I could," Tasha said. "Brian Wu said it was hard, too, so I don't feel too bad."

"What I meant was," Mrs. Gordon continued awkwardly, "do you want to do anything special because of —"

"It's not really a problem, Aunt Elizabeth," Tasha said. "It's the anniversary of my parents' deaths. But like I said before, I've already dealt with my parents' deaths."

"How?" Mrs. Gordon asked.

"By admitting they are dead and getting on with my life." Everyone at the table was silent for a moment.

Mr. Gordon rose from his chair. "To some of us . . . it's a very big thing," he said. "The family is going to church that night. We'll offer our prayers for those who are no longer with us . . ." He looked at Tasha and his face softened. "And our thanks for those who are. You can join us if you want." He set his dishes in the sink and walked out of the room.

"I didn't mean to be casual about it," Tasha said.

"You weren't," Mrs. Gordon said. "It is difficult for us to know what to do or say about all this."

A few minutes later the girls and Mrs. Gordon cleared the table and left the kitchen.

"I guess I blew it downstairs," Tasha told Sarah as they stood in the doorway of Sarah's room. "Uncle Donald is really serious about this thing."

"Dad never really talked about his brother that much. He never told us what he felt or anything."

"So why—"

Sarah raised her hand to cut Tasha off. "When he did mention him, it was always the dumb stuff they did together as kids. Jokes, friends, screwy things. Dad always smiled, or laughed out loud when he talked about the old days. He hasn't told any of those stories since your father died."

"I think it's a family thing," Tasha said. "You know, all those stories about blood being thicker than water and all. My dad and Uncle Donald came from the same roots, the same home."

"Like us," Sarah said.

"Yeah, sort of." Tasha picked up a porcelain elephant from Sarah's dresser and looked at it. "But they were different in a lot of ways, too. Uncle Donald is solid, really solid, and my dad was more exciting, I think."

"I don't know what that's supposed to mean," Sarah said. "I guess your dad really did care for you, maybe more than you thought." There was an edge in her voice.

"Don't get uptight, Sarah." Tasha put the elephant down. "It doesn't mean anything, it's just an observation. Look, I'm tired. See you in the morning."

"Sure," Sarah said. "Sure."

Ten

"I don't believe it!"

Sheryl Johnson was furious. She stood in the gym with Tasha, Naomi, and several other girls from the basketball team. Mrs. Keiser had just made an announcement.

"So Anna Langley is on the team," one girl said nonchalantly. "What's so terrible?"

"Come on," Naomi said. "She can't play ball. We all know that. That Hispanic sister, Sylvia something. She was better."

"Did you go easy on her, Tasha?" Sheryl asked.

"No," Tasha said calmly. "I didn't go easy, but I

didn't go all out, either."

"See!" Sheryl said, throwing up her hands.

"And she sure wasn't better than the girl I went up against," Naomi added. "So why didn't *she* get picked?"

"She was better in a few areas," Joan Gibbons said as she clipped her long blond hair into a bun on top of her head.

"You would say that," Sheryl said sarcastically.

"What's that supposed to mean?" Joan asked.

"Nothing important," Sheryl said. "Let's not start disrespecting each other."

Anna Langley sat on the floor beneath the far basket. She was going through a series of warm-ups, stretching out her legs and arms. But every now and then, Tasha caught her looking their way.

Oh, great, Tasha thought to herself. That's all I need, one more hassle in my life.

Coach Keiser called the team together and gave them her usual pep talk about team spirit and cooperation. She had them welcome Anna into the fold, then had the girls run laps and shoot a few hoops.

It wasn't until halfway through practice that Tasha got a chance to really speak to Anna.

"Like it so far?" Tasha asked.

"What's to like?" Anna dabbed at beads of perspiration on her face.

"Madison. Murphy High," Tasha replied. "I hear you're not from around here."

"And where did you hear that?"

"Talk gets around."

Anna shot a quick glance in the direction of Sheryl and the others. They had formed another little group and occasionally looked over at Anna.

Tasha followed her gaze. "Where are you from?" No answer. "I'm from Oakland, California."

"I'm not," Anna answered.

"What is—"

"Langley, Gordon," the coach called to them. "Get over here. You two are up for some one-on-one."

As they crossed to join Mrs. Keiser, Tasha got the feeling that Anna was not happy about the match-up. She kept glancing from Naomi and Sheryl to Tasha.

"I want to get a better idea of your strengths and weaknesses, Anna," the coach told her. "So you and Tasha mix it up a little. OK, let's go."

Once again Tasha found herself whipping around the court with Anna. But this time it was worse. Anna was even more aggressive. Several times she bumped into Tasha, hard. Mrs. Keiser called out warnings and instructions, telling Anna that moves like that would cost the team in a game. But Anna didn't seem to be listening.

Tasha began playing less for points and more for revenge. It became a grudge match.

They moved with speed and strength. Tasha sank several baskets in a row. She out-dribbled Anna and out-jumped her when taking a shot. Anna became even more agitated. When she got the ball she started taking wild shots and rushing in for the rebounds.

The team cheered for Tasha from the sidelines. Sheryl and Naomi made several wisecracks about Anna's playing. Mrs. Keiser reprimanded them, but Anna played even harder.

"Eat her up, Tasha!" Sheryl called out.

Tasha started from behind the foul line. She looked at Anna. She was sweating and out of breath. Tasha straightened up and beckoned to her. Anna's face went from tired to grimly determined as she came out to where Tasha stood with the ball.

Tasha dribbled once to her right, brought the ball through her legs on a low dribble, took a step to the right, and went easily around Anna to the left. From the bench the other girls cheered.

Anna took the ball out and missed an off-balance shot, and Tasha got the rebound. She worked her way slowly toward the basket. Twisting and weaving, she finally whirled and leaped into the air. Tasha was certain her shot would go in with ease. But suddenly Anna flew through the air, her hand stretched high to block the shot. They slammed together in midair and Tasha went crashing to the floor. A stabbing pain shot through her left wrist and the air whooshed out of her body, like she might black out.

"Let me have a look at that," Coach Keiser said as she and the team crowded around Tasha. "It's not broken, since you can move it. I'd say you have a bad sprain. Have it checked out," she said finally. "Now, tell me what was going on out there." There was a hard tone to Coach Keiser's voice. And all eyes fell on Anna.

"Nothing," Anna said. She looked around at the others, then at Tasha.

"I guess I got a little excited," Tasha said.

"You both did," the coach replied. "And I won't have any showboating on my team. From any players. Now let's clean up and change. See you Wednesday."

"If one of us had pulled what Anna did, we'd be off the team," Sheryl whispered as they headed for the lockers. "Can't figure out why she got picked in the first place."

"I don't like her," Naomi said bitterly.

"You think you would have done better?" Tasha asked.

"She almost broke your wrist!" Naomi said.

"Right, but I was on out there today," Tasha said. "If you can't see why she made the team you're blind. It's got to do with a lot more than color."

Eleven

The school nurse confirmed Coach Keiser's suspicion. Tasha's wrist was sprained.

"Go easy on it for the next few days," the nurse told Tasha. She wrapped an Ace bandage around the wrist.

"But I have practice!" Tasha protested.

"You can watch, sweetheart, but don't participate." The nurse was firm, and Tasha left her office feeling worse than when she had entered.

"Thank you, Anna Langley," she muttered as she walked out onto the front steps of the school.

It was just four o'clock and Tasha knew the gang

was probably still at 18 Pine, but she didn't feel like seeing them right now. She also wasn't ready to go home. She zipped up her parka and simply started walking.

The cool air felt good on her face. Now and then a breeze came up and gently rustled the trees along the avenue.

Her mind kept replaying the events of the past week, and it was a dismal picture. First she had decided to enter the math competition. What had prompted that move, she wondered. Had it been jealousy? Had she been so tired of hearing everyone praise Sarah? Or had it been the letter from Oakland?

Tasha stopped in front of a toy store. Through the large window she could see a number of people browsing, among them a father and daughter. The little girl was about six or seven, with expressive eyes. She was using them to get her father to buy her a huge teddy bear.

Memories flooded Tasha's mind. It was a warm summer day, ten years ago, in Montreal. One of the rare times her father had taken her and her mother on a team trip.

She had been walking with her parents, sightseeing, when she spotted a small toy shop, tucked away on a narrow street. The owner had looked like a skinny Santa Claus, and the shop had smelled like wood and sweet spices.

On a shelf behind the counter sat a beautiful porcelain doll. It was dressed in the Victorian style, in a powder-blue dress with lots of white petticoats underneath and a matching blue bonnet. The owner wanted sixty dollars for the doll. Her mother said absolutely no. She told Tasha that she had enough toys, and certainly enough dolls.

But Tasha wanted that doll. She smiled and blinked her huge brown eyes at her father, as she had always done. And finally he said, "You can never have enough of the things you really want." He bought her the doll and she slept with it the whole time they were in Montreal, and she brought it back home. That had been the most precious gift, the most special time.

Tasha's eyes began to sting as she fought back the urge to cry. She couldn't remember where the doll was now. In fact, she hadn't seen it in years.

She turned and walked quickly away.

PINE

Twelve

On Tuesday, the results of the math test were posted outside the math office. Tasha stood with Cindy Phillips, reading the notice.

"You're number three!" Cindy said, punching Tasha's arm. "Number three in the county!"

"All right!" Sarah looked down the list. Brian Wu was number five, and two other students from Murphy High had made the top ten.

"You're amazing!" Cindy said.

"True, true," Tasha said happily.

Cindy continued to be Tasha's personal cheerleader until third period started and they walked into math class.

"Your score was *very* remarkable, Miss Gordon," Mr. Cala said once the class had settled down. "Not what I had expected at all."

"Were you surprised?" Tasha didn't try to hide her sarcasm.

"More than surprised." Mr. Cala walked around the desk. "I spoke to Mr. Olsen, the monitor. He said you seemed to have problems on the test. You had to leave every so often to go to the bathroom."

"I managed," Tasha said.

"Yes, and we'll be seeing about that," he told her. "There were some very serious young men in that competition, and they are trying quite hard to advance their educations. This certainly isn't the time or the place for frivolities or stunts."

"Stunts?"

Mr. Cala turned his back to her and started to write math formulas on the blackboard.

"Stunts?" Tasha repeated.

"The discussion," Mr. Cala said without turning toward Tasha, "is over...for now."

Tasha felt frustrated. She couldn't tell if Mr. Cala was angry because he'd been wrong or because she had done well on the test.

"It's probably a combination of both," April said when they had settled into their favorite booth at 18 Pine Street. "Some people are just sore losers."

"Sore loser or not, he made me furious," Tasha

said. "Especially the way he said, 'the discussion is over *for now.*' "

"There's Billy at the counter," April said. "You want me to leave so he'll come over here?"

"Child, if you're going to play Cupid, then get out your arrows, walk over to Mr. Turner, and tell him to get his buns over here right now."

"Well, yes, ma'am," April said, standing. She slid out of the booth and over to Billy.

Tasha saw April whisper into Billy's ear, and she turned her head away before Billy got to the booth.

"You summoned?" he said, getting ready to sit.

"Don't sit," Tasha said. "Just pick me up in an hour and take me someplace wonderful."

"I don't have any wonderful money," Billy said.

"What do you have?"

Billy looked into his pockets and counted some change. "One dollar and nine cents," he said. "Not too cool, huh?"

"I have movie money if you're interested," Tasha said.

"Hey, we're on," Billy answered. "Five OK?"

"Fine, now go get April and tell her to come back here so I can tell her my troubles."

Tasha knew that telling April her troubles with Mr. Cala wouldn't help, and she didn't want to tell her about how she was beginning to feel about Billy. But she did like April and wanted to talk to somebody besides Billy at the moment. Maybe she would tell April about how sore her wrist was.

April came back with two slices and pushed one toward Tasha.

"I am now going to tell you about my sore wrist," Tasha said. "And how tired I am of having a sore wrist."

"I don't want to hear about your stupid wrist," April said, pulling back the slice of pizza. "Tell me about you and Billy."

"Billy?" Tasha said, pulling back the slice. "The boy means nothing to me at all, darling, nothing to me at all."

It's only a movie, Tasha told herself as she showered and shampooed her hair. So why the big rush? She applied her eyeliner and shadow carefully, put on her favorite perfume, a pair of jeans, knee-high boots, and a silky, cream-colored blouse. It felt soft to the touch.

It's only a movie date, she repeated as she viewed the full effect in the mirror. But somehow it felt like much, much more. She decided not to wear the Ace bandage. I'll be careful, she told herself. Besides, it ruins the effect of the outfit. And we can't have that.

The movie was a love story. All around her Tasha could sense the tension as the couple crossed the line between being friends and lovers.

When the film was over there was a strange tension between her and Billy. A sense of anticipation.

Leaving the theater, Billy drove them to a burger place, where they picked up some takeout food, then parked at the far end of the parking lot.

The windows began to fog up as they sat there talking. The darkness closed in on them, and for a time it seemed like there was no one else in the world.

"I had a nice time," Tasha told Billy as she fed him a french fry. They were close, facing each other, watching each other as they spoke.

Tasha felt anxious, yet somehow at ease.

"You're really something." Billy's arm slipped down along her shoulder.

"What am I?"

"Crazy wild one minute, soft and ..." Billy seemed to search for the word with no luck. "I don't know." He gave her a sip of his soda.

"Do you like me?" Tasha's voice was soft, tentative. She didn't know why she had asked the question. Then again, maybe she did.

"You know I like you. I mean, a guy would have to be stupid not to." He moved closer. "And I'm not that stupid."

Suddenly they were kissing. Tasha felt a wave of emotions wash over her. She felt his arms around her, his fingers running through her hair.

It was just like the movie. She had found her man, and they were together. She heard the heroine of the movie saying the romantic lines in her head.

PINE

Thirteen

Tasha heard another voice, her mother's voice: *Respect yourself, girl! When no one else does, or when everyone does. You've got to respect yourself first.* She froze.

A moment later, Billy sensed the change and pulled back. "What's wrong, Tasha?"

"It's not the right time, it's not the right place."

"Am I the wrong guy?" he asked.

"I don't know," she admitted. "But there is a better time to ask that question."

"I hear you." Billy leaned back against the seat and stared out the window.

"Are you angry with me?" she asked.

"I don't think so. I guess I'm just disappointed." He looked away.

"In me? You feel I led you on?"

"No, that's not what I'm saying." Billy turned to face her. "I'm disappointed in myself. I mean I thought I had my head on straight about a lot of things—especially something serious like this. But here I am, making the major moves on you in a car, in a parking lot! I mean, where was my head?"

Tasha squeezed his hand. "The same place mine was, I'll bet."

Billy nodded. "Maybe. So what do we do now?"

"I'd like to get to know you better," she said. "But I also need to get to know myself. I think that's going to take some time. I don't know how much, or where I'll wind up."

"Or with whom," Billy said. Tasha nodded. "So why don't we agree to hang out a little, take all the time we need, and"—he chuckled and rubbed his forehead. "I don't believe I'm going to say this, but—we can be..."

"Friends?" Tasha said with a smile.

Billy nodded and they both burst into laughter.

"You'd better get me home now. I still have a lot of homework to do."

"Got to be that way?" Billy asked.

"Got to be."

"I'm in pain," he said.

"Better your pain," Tasha said, "than a disaster. Right?"

"Well..."

They drove to the Gordon house in silence. When they arrived, Tasha pushed the car door open and got out. Billy got out of the driver's side and walked her to the door.

At the door she gave him a warm good-bye kiss which left a puzzled expression on his face.

"I said friends, Billy, not brother and sister."

Fourteen

Once inside, Tasha said hello to Mrs. Gordon and Miss Essie, who were sitting in the living room. "Sorry I missed dinner," she said as she walked by.

She found Mr. Gordon in the den. He was sitting in the dark, staring into space.

"Uncle Donald."

Mr. Gordon was startled. "Sorry, I didn't hear you come in."

Tasha hesitated. "You got a moment?"

He saw the worried look on her face. "Is something wrong?"

"Nothing and everything. Can we go for a walk?"

Donald Gordon rose from his chair and placed an

arm around Tasha's shoulder. "North or south?"

They strolled slowly down the avenue. The evening air was chilly, and a biting wind seemed to cut into them now and then. But on they walked, past old colonial-style houses, down past the elementary school, and around the park.

It was mostly small talk at first, about school, work, the math contest. But finally, as they stood beside the duck pond, Tasha looked up at her uncle. "Why didn't you come for me sooner?"

Mr. Gordon dug his hands into his coat pockets and took a deep breath. "Your father and I...James and I were brothers. I mean not just in body, but in spirit. At first we were close. Being older, I'd show him how to do things. I'd be the one to look after him when we went places with our folks. I was punished first, and I was the one who went without a lot of things. Our folks felt if they gave me too much, James would feel slighted."

"What if they gave him things?"

"I would understand, because I was older. At least, that's what they said."

"Did Miss Essie and Granddad play favorites?"

"No. Maybe. It didn't matter. James had the gift. Charm. Magic. People were drawn to him. What he wanted he usually got."

Tasha knew what her uncle meant. She had seen that charm in action all her life. Her father's teammates, reporters, fans, even her own friends, seemed to fawn all over him. Her mother had once told Tasha, "You're very much like him. You can draw people in." At the time Tasha had taken that as a compliment. Now she wasn't so sure.

"As we got older, James excelled in sports and drew even more adoration from our friends and family. He was written up in the school and local papers, and near graduation from high school he had six universities offering him full scholarships.

"So off he went. And when times got hard he sent money. And when birthdays or anniversaries came up, he sent money. And when he came home to visit, once or twice, he talked about himself, and he *spent* money."

"Were you jealous?"

"I was envious, sweetheart," Mr. Gordon answered with some sadness. "I had barely gotten a scholarship to college. I had to hold down three jobs and study. Plus I was the one around whenever my folks needed something. Care, company, or just someone to criticize. James was gone, good old Donald was right there all the time. Even after I graduated.

"I could have enjoyed James's successes more if he had only shown some sense of caring about what was happening back home. But he was always off somewhere, doing something more important.

"Finally, eight years ago, Dad was dying and I called James. It wasn't the first heart attack he had suffered, so James says, 'I'm going to an award ceremony tonight and I'll call when I get home.' " Mr. Gordon stopped walking and turned to Tasha. "He didn't get home until three A.M. Dad had died at midnight."

101

"I'm sorry," was all Tasha could say. She felt a tightening in her throat. She felt angry and embarrassed.

"When James arrived for the funeral, I...We had some harsh words. We didn't speak much after that. Lord knows Elizabeth and your mother tried to get us to make up, but we were both too stubborn. Even Miss Essie tried to get me to forgive and forget, but I wanted no part of it.

"Four years later, James and your mother died. And I didn't know what to say or do. Your mother's people said they wanted you out there, and that you would be happier staying in a place you knew, with people you knew. So I guess I took the easy way out."

"You must have really hated my father."

"No, sweetheart. I really loved him."

Tasha suddenly threw herself into her uncle's arms and held on as tight as she could. "I once asked him who he admired most. And he said... 'my brother.' I never asked him why."

"It's getting colder," Mr. Gordon said. "Maybe we should start heading back."

"Uncle Donald." Tasha clung to his hand with all her strength. "Am I really like my father?"

Mr. Gordon smiled. "You're charming, outgoing, intelligent, and aggressive. In those ways, you are exactly like him. But I've seen you with Sarah. I've watched your relationship grow. And in many ways I would say you are very much your own person."

"I'm so confused right now."

"We all are," Mr. Gordon said gently.

"I still miss them," Tasha said tearfully.

"I know."

"And sometimes I feel so angry with them," she admitted.

"They left you," Mr. Gordon said thoughtfully. "They left us and we had so much to say to them."

"Yes," Tasha said.

"You still can, in a way."

"I know what you mean. Prayer and stuff."

"That, and by living your life and speaking your mind. Remember, some part of them lives on through you. Deeds are a way of speaking to them. It's like saying, Hey! I'm OK, and I remember."

"Am I your way of talking to them? To my father?"

"You're my way of holding on to a part of him I had lost. His gift of life," Mr. Gordon replied. "But more important, you are family. And that is precious above all else."

Tasha felt a shiver run through her. "Thank you, Uncle Donald."

"For what?"

"For being there. And for being here."

They walked back to the house hand in hand. Tasha listened as he told her a funny story about her dad as a child. She enjoyed it all the more because her uncle was laughing, too.

Fifteen

Tasha stood in Sarah's doorway, interrupting her cousin on the phone.

"It's Jennifer," Sarah explained. "She says she's feeling better, but she sounds like a chain saw underwater."

"Tell her I said hi." Tasha stepped into the room and fidgeted at the foot of Sarah's bed, like a small child.

"Jen, I've got to go," Sarah said after watching her cousin for a few moments. "Either Tasha has some really exciting news to tell me, or Allison's locked her out of the bathroom." Sarah hung up the phone and turned to her cousin. "Cindy and I went to the Community Center today, just to set up our schedules. We saw Mr. Tanner and Kenny," she said.

"Tell me all about it later," Tasha said. "Let me tell you about tonight. You know I went out with Billy," she began. "Well, we saw a great movie. Then we went to Fat Burgers and parked in their lot." Tasha paused. "One thing led to another and—"

"You didn't?" Sarah's eyes grew wide.

"No, I didn't. We came close, but I couldn't and Billy was cool with that."

Sarah was amazed. "He was?"

"Yes," Tasha replied wistfully. "In fact, he was an angel. But what I really wanted to tell you about is something completely different. I need your help."

"With Billy?" Sarah asked.

"With a lot of things. I've got a lot to learn about myself and where I'm going. I've been confused a little about . . . *things*. But I know I'll need the help of my friends and my family. That's you both times." Tasha's eyes misted over.

Sarah took Tasha's hands. "Don't worry, cousin, you're stuck with this branch of the Gordons and we're stuck with you."

"You mean that?"

"Believe it!" Sarah smiled.

"OK, then," Tasha said, jumping up and heading for the door, "join me in my room. I've got some studying to do."

A sudden scream came from Allison's room. The two girls looked at each other and raced into the hallway. Mr. Gordon was already coming up the stairs.

"I hate school!" was the next cry from Allison's room, and they all stopped dead in their tracks. It's only Allison having one of her weekly snit fits, Tasha thought. Mr. Gordon started back downstairs. Sarah and Tasha went to Sarah's room first, then down the hall to see Allison.

They found her sitting on her bed brooding. A half-finished report lay on her desk, next to several opened books and a small pile of crumpled papers.

"Are you still mad at us for not writing your report for you?" Tasha asked as she and Sarah slipped into the room.

"I want to be," Allison replied.

Tasha sat down on the bed, next to Allison, and set a pile of books on the floor. "How's the report going?"

"Terrible," was Allison's only reply.

Sarah picked up the report and read the first page. "Looks to me like you started off all right, then you—"

"Got stuck, bored, dumber than dirt!" Allison exclaimed.

"You are not dumb," Tasha insisted. "You're related to us and we're brilliant."

Allison flopped over on to her stomach. "Get real."

"We are," Tasha said, "and you're not dumb. Weird maybe, but not dumb."

"So," Sarah said, grabbing up some loose-leaf paper. "Who is Phillis Wheatley?"

Allison frowned. "I don't know. Some new kid at your school?"

Sarah and Tasha smiled. "Try an ex-slave, and a self-educated poet," Sarah said.

"Writing and being published in America at a time most blacks were still tilling soil and planting cotton," Tasha added.

Allison sat up on her bed, her eyes keen with interest.

"Then there's Maya Angelou," Sarah said. "She wrote *I Know Why the Caged Bird Sings*."

"I saw the movie," Allison said doubtfully.

"Well, she also writes poetry," Tasha said, producing one of the books she and Sarah had brought with them, "and she has lectured and read these poems all over the world."

"Then there's Nikki Giovanni, Lucille Clifton, and Langston Hughes." Tasha called out the names as she picked up books from the floor.

"What we're trying to tell you," Sarah told Allison, "is there are hundreds of poets out there. Many are very good. And just maybe your report might be more interesting to you if you can connect with the people you write about."

"You mean Whitman and Frost are boring, right?"

"Wrong." Sarah corrected her little sister. "They've written some beautiful pieces."

"Their poetry speaks to a lot of people, including me," Tasha said. "But sometimes you need to hear other voices." She opened one of the books. "We'll read you some of the things we got from the library. Then we'll see."

"All right," Allison said. "But don't make any bets."

For the next half hour, Tasha and Sarah took turns reading aloud the works they had brought. The more they read, the more animated they became.

The poems covered so many aspects of life: love, men, women, city rhythms, country sun, seasons, birth and death.

Tasha began strutting around the room when the poem's voice was that of a sassy, brassy woman. Sarah slipped into a Southern accent to read one piece, sitting on the windowsill and speaking quietly.

"That was great," Allison told her sister.

Finally the girls read some poems by Frost and Whitman, and Allison was amazed at how much she had missed the first time.

"My mom used to read poetry to me when I was a kid," Tasha told them. "I don't know if I got all of it, either. But I liked the sound of her voice." Tasha paused. "I'd forgotten that," she said softly.

"So," Sarah said to Allison. "Can we write this thing now?"

"*I* can," her sister replied. She jumped to the desk, grabbed her pen, then stopped. "It would be easier if you guys could stay around for a while. Just until I get through the hard parts."

Tasha and Sarah pushed aside some of the mess on Allison's bed and floor and made themselves comfortable.

Sixteen

Tasha awoke Wednesday morning feeling charged with excitement. The day felt good, and the sun was bursting through her bedroom window. A noisy blue jay chirped outside the window and, opening it, she joyfully sang back.

Tasha ran around the room selecting her clothes and accessories. She decided to wear her white pants and an off-white sweater. Despite her problems with Mr. Cala, and the anniversary of her parents' death, she had decided to meet the day with a positive feeling.

"You're on top of the world this morning," Mrs. Gordon said as Tasha entered the kitchen.

"I feel like I taught the birds to fly and Hammer how

to dance." Tasha grabbed her aunt and twirled her around the floor.

Mrs. Gordon laughed. "Who is this new guy in your life?"

"It's not about a new guy, Aunt Elizabeth. I just feel good about *me*."

"Package that feeling and we could save the world." Mrs. Gordon picked up her breakfast dishes and took them to the sink. "Your uncle and I are very, very proud of your score on the math test."

Tasha felt uneasy. "Me too," she said softly as she poured herself a glass of juice. "I'm supposed to hear about the scholarships today. I'm glad I was able to show Mr. Cala that a woman can do as well in math as a man—I hope he gets my message."

"You can do anything you put your mind to, Tasha."

"Where's Uncle Donald?" Tasha asked, her good mood restored.

"He had to go in early, something about reports that were due last week." Mrs. Gordon made a sour face.

"He doesn't like that part of school, does he?" Tasha said, putting more bread into the toaster.

Mrs. Gordon shook her head. "I don't envy him," she said sympathetically. "But B-O-R-I-N-G is part of W-O-R-K for most people. That's just the way it is."

Tasha suddenly hugged her aunt very tightly. "You guys are the greatest."

Mrs. Gordon chuckled. "Why do you say that, sweetheart?"

"Because you care, I mean *really* care," Tasha

replied. "I knew a lot of people who were into what Mom called *lip service*. Say much, do nothing. That's not you and Uncle Donald."

"We try, sugar, we try."

"Wow!" Tasha exclaimed as she noticed the wall clock. "I've got to get to school."

"Do you want a lift? Sarah and I will be leaving in about twenty minutes."

"No, thanks," Tasha answered. She gulped down her juice and grabbed an apple from the fruit bowl. "Sarah's dragging around up there, and I want to get to school early enough to see Mrs. Keiser." She gingerly flexed her wrist.

"How is that doing?"

"Better. But I'm anxious to get back to practice before I lose my edge."

"Somehow, sweetheart, I have trouble believing that will ever happen."

Tasha was at the door when Mrs. Gordon called to her. "I just wanted to say...We're going to Heavenly Grace Church tonight at eight." Tasha looked down at the ground.

"I'm not saying you have to come with us," her aunt continued. "But the invitation is there if you want to."

"Thanks," Tasha replied a bit too quickly. "I'll see you later."

As Tasha boarded the public bus that stopped near Murphy High, her thoughts were jumbled. She appreciated what the family was trying to do, but she didn't want to take part in any ceremonies. I've dealt with all of this, she told herself. I'm fine. Now I need to establish myself. I need to feel good about Tasha Gordon. And that means dealing with Mr. Cala.

"Miss Gordon," Mr. Cala said sternly, "I would like to see you in the math office."

The first thought that came to Tasha was that Mr. Cala was going to talk about scholarships. She knew he was going to talk about the math test. He was going to try to make her feel as if she were lucky, she thought. Maybe if she got up the nerve she would tell him that she *was* lucky, lucky to be smart.

"Sit down," he said.

Tasha sat.

"I've been reviewing your actual test papers," Mr. Cala said. "You didn't show such in-depth knowledge in the classroom quizzes."

"I wasn't as prepared for them," Tasha replied. An uneasy feeling began to sweep over her as she faced the math teacher.

"That was obvious, but your so-called performance on this test gave you a score that, for you, was remarkable." Mr. Cala eyed her steadily. "Your work in class has been passable. But the math test questions were trickier. They were devised to confound boys who really *live* math. You do not."

"Boys who—"

"Lack of proof prevents me from making a direct accusation. But I'll say this much," Mr. Cala said as he methodically gathered up his things, "I am aware that

114

you left the room during both parts of the test. I also have it from reliable sources that you have been asking about small, hand-held computers."

"Whoa! Wait a minute!"

"I am also aware that the test was given in a school whose principal may hold some sympathy toward you. He is your uncle?"

"What has that to got to do with anything?" Tasha was in shock. She heard her words come out softly, slowly. Mr. Cala didn't have to go on. Tasha already knew what he was saying.

"Men, especially relatives, are often motivated to make things easier for a young woman, one who might be in over her head."

"My uncle didn't—"

Mr. Cala dismissed her protest with a leisurely wave of his hand. "I am recommending to the County Board of Education that you be retested."

White-hot rage flashed through Tasha's body. She almost couldn't speak. But finally words came to her. "You're accusing me and my uncle of cheating! Why aren't you *man* enough to say it!"

Mr. Cala was unruffled. "I'm not accusing you of anything. I'm simply suggesting to the school board that they may, in the interest of fairness, wish to retest you. Of course, if you are really this good in math, you won't have a problem, will you?"

"You are *implying* that my uncle gave me a computer to use on the test!" Tasha could barely keep herself from screaming at the teacher. "I know you don't think much of me, Mr. Cala. But don't you ever accuse Uncle Donald of anything like that, ever! He's an ethical man, Mr. Cala. I suggest you look that word up."

She whirled around and stormed out of the room.

In the hallway she bumped into Anna Langley. Their eyes locked. Anna looked surprised, then defiant.

Tasha felt ready to explode. And she knew if they exchanged even one word it would lead to a fight neither of them would win. She ran down the hallway and ducked into a stairwell.

She leaned her head against the wall. The cool tile helped to calm her down a bit. But she was still flushed with anger, and tears welled up in her eyes.

Tasha had been accused of some things in her life, but never of cheating. She had always done well in school, and it had never occurred to her to cheat at anything.

Now a teacher was all but saying outright that she had cheated. And he was implicating her uncle. Something like this could seriously hurt Uncle Donald's reputation, she told herself.

Tasha suddenly felt all of her confidence drain out of her. There, in the empty, echoing stairwell, she felt as alone as she ever had. It just isn't fair, she thought. It just isn't fair.

Seventeen

Tasha was in the library looking for articles on the ozone layer when she saw April Winter peer in through the glass doors. April's face was red, and by her determined stride and the way she held her books across her chest, Tasha knew that April was mad.

"It's all over the school!" April said.

"About Mr. Cala?" Tasha looked up from the computer index she had been using.

"What else!" April's chin stuck out.

"Okay, get everybody together in the cafeteria," Tasha said. "Sit by the window if you can. We'll come up with something."

117

"You bet we will!" April spun on one foot and stomped out of the library.

A strike. That was Tasha's first thought of what to do about Mr. Cala. The whole school would go on a strike to protest his being such a pigheaded sexist. She would get Kwame and Billy to paint signs, and maybe some of the cheerleaders would lead a parade around the school. It was a great idea.

She would get Jennifer to call the newspapers. Jennifer had written press releases before, and Tasha remembered that Jennifer's mother knew someone on the local paper.

By the time she got to the cafeteria Tasha was already envisioning the story being picked up by all the newspapers in the country.

There was a tight crowd in front of the lunchroom window. Through the tangle of arms and legs Tasha saw that someone was in the middle, and that Cindy had her arms around her. It had to be Sarah. That was natural, Tasha thought. After all, it was her father whom Mr. Cala had accused of cheating.

"Sarah, don't worry," Tasha said as she approached her cousin. "We can handle this thing. I've got some dynamite ideas."

"Tasha, how could you?" Sarah was obviously upset. "How could you cheat on a test like this?"

"What?" Tasha couldn't believe what she was hearing.

"Is that why you wanted to know about Kwame's calculator?" Brian Wu asked. "To cheat?"

"I didn't cheat!" Tasha looked at the sea of faces around her. "I didn't cheat!"

"Tasha, we want to believe you," Cindy said. "But you've never been that good at math."

"I've always done well in math," Tasha protested.

"Not *that* well, Miss Gordon." Mr. Cala's voice cut through the crowd. He was cafeteria monitor this period and had seen the commotion. "But just to give you a chance to redeem yourself—"

"Redeem myself?" Tasha stood up and looked at all her friends gathered around her cousin. "Redeem myself from what?"

"The county board has given you permission to retake the test." Mr. Cala's voice rose slightly. "Then we can see exactly how well you can do."

"I'm not going to take the test again," Tasha said. "That would be like . . . like. . . ."

"Like proving you're that good," Brian said.

"I've already proven it!" Tasha felt tears stinging her eyes. "I've already proven it!"

She felt herself half stumbling, half running from the cafeteria. She had to get away, to think about what was going on. How could they believe, even think, that she was cheating?

Her afternoon classes went by in a blur. Several times she found herself crying. None of the teachers had to ask why. They had all heard the story. And from their tone, Tasha thought many of them believed she had cheated.

She decided to pretend everything was normal. She

told herself that she would forget about what had happened, make believe that it was all a bad dream.

She still had a lot of thinking to do, though, and after school she decided to go to the gym. A good sweat always seemed to clear her mind.

Anna Langley was in the gym, throwing the basketball against the backboard, catching it and pushing it back up quickly. Tasha didn't feel like talking to Anna, but the girl was there.

"Heard about them saying you were cheating," Anna said.

"So?"

Anna shrugged without looking at her. "So, I don't believe you were cheating."

"You don't know me," Tasha said. She dribbled down one side of the lane and shot the ball softly against the backboard. "You don't know what I might do. You're just running your mouth."

"I know you work too hard at what you do to mess it up by cheating," Anna said. "I've heard about you. You do everything hard. You play soccer hard, you play basketball hard, and you probably worked hard to pass that math test. I'm just like you."

"You're like me?" Tasha put the ball on her hip.

"Yup." Anna nodded. "I might not be as good as you, but I work as hard as you do."

"Hey, look, we got off on the wrong foot," Tasha said, as she sat down.

"Did we?"

"It started out hostile," Tasha pointed out. "That

seems like the wrong foot to me."

"I give what I get," Anna replied stubbornly.

"I guess the team's been giving you a hard time?"

"I can take it. I don't need your sympathy," Anna said.

"We're both good at giving attitude." Tasha smiled. "In fact, I'm reigning queen in these parts."

Anna fought back a grin. "I don't know about that. Naomi's pretty good at dishing it out, too."

"Naomi is good people once you get to know her," Tasha said. "And once she gets to know you."

"Fat chance."

"Look, you're on the team now. That means we work together or we don't work at all. My dad was a stickler for that rule."

"Your dad was James Gordon, wasn't he?" Anna said. "Defensive end, tremendous record throughout his career—"

Tasha was amazed. "How did you know that?"

"People talk about you," Anna admitted. "You have a reputation around here."

Tasha shook her head. "That's news to me." She flexed her wrist gingerly.

"Does that still hurt?" Anna asked with sincere concern.

"Not really. I think I'll be back at practice soon."

Anna fingered her hair nervously. "I'm sorry about that. I wasn't thinking and—"

"Hey." Tasha cut her off. "It was my fault, too. We both lost our heads. My reason was ego-on-the-loose.

What was yours?"

"Overdose of idiot pills. I guess I was trying to prove something," Anna said sadly.

"Like what?" Tasha asked.

"I don't know," Anna replied slowly. "I'm new to Madison. Hey, let me ask you something. You going to take the test over again?"

"I don't know," Tasha said. "I'm thinking about it."

"See, I told you we're alike. You're going to prove yourself, right?"

"You proving yourself?"

"In a way. I'm from a small town in Kansas. My dad worked for a big company out there. The plant went bust, so they transferred him here to their east coast offices." Anna hesitated for a moment. She stared at Tasha as if studying her. Finally she said, "There weren't too many black people in my town."

Tasha didn't say a word.

"When I got here ... and saw all these different types of people, I got, well, I ..."

"You got uncomfortable?"

Anna nodded. "I figured I'd never make it on the team because there were so many black kids. I mean you know those idiots who are always saying that blacks are better at sports, that kind of thing."

"And boys are better at math," Tasha said. She shot the ball, watched as it swished easily through the basket.

"Yeah, something like that," Anna said.

"Maybe I won't take the test again," Tasha said.

"Maybe I'll make them either put up or shut up."

Anna was silent for a moment. "When are you coming back to practice?"

"The nurse says another few days to be safe."

"Good," Anna replied. "It will be good to have a ... friend on the team."

"Tell me about it," Tasha said as she headed for the locker room. "Tell me about it."

After the workout, Tasha put her things in her locker and took a long, slow walk to 18 Pine. She didn't go in. She stood outside the window for a long while, looking at her own sad reflection in the window, and then turned and started home.

"Tasha!" It was Kwame.

"Yes," Tasha said coolly, "did you call me?"

"Yeah," Kwame said. "Look, I just want you to know that I'm sorry about what happened. I know you didn't cheat."

"How do you know?" Sarah asked.

"It's just something I believe in my heart," Kwame said.

"Everybody else thinks I cheated," Tasha said. "Sarah does. Cindy does."

"I'm not everybody else," Kwame said.

Tasha felt a new flood of tears in the works, and moved closer to Kwame. She kissed him gently on the forehead. "Thanks, buddy."

"Look, why don't you come on in to 18 Pine," Kwame said. "Anybody that wants to mess with you has to mess with me first. And if Brian Wu says anything to you, I'll punch his lights out."

"Kwame, you can't beat Brian," Tasha said.

"Yeah, well, for you I'd try, Tasha," Kwame said.

"Thanks, but I think I'll go on home," Tasha said.

"Oh, yeah, if you see April, try to calm her down," Kwame said. "She was so mad at Mr. Cala she wanted to find where he lived and complain to his wife."

"He's married?"

"Nope, lives with his mother," Kwame said.

"Poor woman," Tasha said, turning toward home. "Thanks a lot, Kwame."

It was better going home after talking to Kwame and hearing about April. It was nice knowing who your real friends were. Friends who would be there in a pinch.

Tasha arrived home about five o'clock. Allison was in the bathroom filling a balloon with water.

"I'm trying to see when the balloon will pop," she said happily.

"Just when you need it the most," Tasha said. "Believe me."

Tasha walked into the kitchen and greeted her uncle, who was sitting at the table. He had a cup of coffee in front of him and a yellow pad. Mrs. Gordon was leaning against the sink counter. Allison walked in and sat down at the other side of the table.

"Dad's writing all the things he can do to Mr. Cala for calling you a cheat," Allison said.

"Why didn't you tell us what had happened?" Mr.

Gordon said. "Sarah told us."

"I didn't know what you were going to think, Uncle Donald," Tasha said, first putting her sneakers on the chair and then pushing them off onto the tiled kitchen floor. "I needed some time to think it through."

Sarah came into the kitchen and quietly sat down in the corner.

"Did he say it in front of anybody?" Mr. Gordon asked.

Tasha noticed that Sarah had been crying.

"I think he's said it in front of everybody with two ears," Tasha said. "The whole school knows about it."

"And I just can't figure out why Sarah wasn't more supportive. Why she didn't mention it to us if you didn't. I had to hear it from the county board," Mr. Gordon said.

"What did they say?" Tasha asked. Out of the corner of her eye she saw that Sarah had her head down.

"They told me what Mr. Cala had said." A vein in Mr. Gordon's neck stuck out over his shirt. He was talking quietly, but was obviously upset. "They said he had no proof, and said they would not require you to take the test over again, but that you could if you chose to. They also mentioned that Mr. Cala thought the test being held in the school where I'm the principal had something to do with your doing so well. I feel like—"

"Donald!" Mrs. Gordon spoke sharply to her husband. "Getting violent won't help."

"It might," Mr. Gordon muttered under his breath.

"Tasha, honey, you need to know that your uncle and

125

I are standing behind you on this," Mrs. Gordon said. "We don't believe you cheated, and we'll do everything necessary to back you up—even if it means taking Mr. Cala to court for slandering you. You are too smart and too talented to have your reputation smeared like this."

By this time Sarah was crying. Tasha could see her body shake as she sobbed. Tasha walked around the table and put her arms around her cousin.

"I just don't see how Sarah could have . . . " Mr. Gordon shook his head and looked away.

"Everybody was saying I cheated," Tasha said, coming to Sarah's defense. "I guess I would have believed it, too, if I didn't know I didn't cheat." Tasha was surprised at herself. She had been angry with Sarah—really angry. She couldn't understand why her cousin had abandoned her the way she had. But when she looked at her and saw how upset she was, she knew that Sarah was as miserable about what had happened as she was.

"That's not true," Sarah said. She lifted her tear-streaked face. "You could never cheat, Tasha. I realized that as soon as I thought about it. It was just that you are so good at everything, I was hoping you'd fail for once."

"Sarah, what a terrible thing to say!" Mrs. Gordon looked very sad.

"No, it's not," Allison said. "I know this boy in the fifth grade who won every game in the schoolyard three days in a row and got an A in history and Rodney Abernathy punched him right in the face."

"Those are children," Mr. Gordon said. "Sarah is not a child. She should know better."

"Rodney Abernathy is in the fifth grade and he's eleven—" Allison said.

"Allison, we're not talking about Rodney Abernathy. We're talking about your sister."

Allison folded her arms and pouted.

"So Sarah made a mistake," Tasha said. "Big deal. Aren't families entitled to make mistakes once in a while?"

"Yes, but..." Mr. Gordon sputtered. "How do you want to handle this? Should we go in and talk to him? You want to sue him? Have him assassinated?"

"No," Tasha said. "I'll just ace his class. That'll tick him off."

"Are you sure?" Mrs. Gordon asked.

"I'm sure," Tasha said. "Say, wasn't this family going to church tonight?"

"I don't know," Mr. Gordon. "I think I might be too mad to go to church."

"Then maybe we *should* go," Mrs. Gordon said.

Eighteen

Heavenly Grace Church stood on the corner of Cyprus and Hawkins avenues. It was a small building made of stone and stained glass. Red oak doors opened into a small vestibule with a tile floor. A few steps led to a beautiful chapel.

On the altar, a number of long, thick candles flickered, throwing off warm beams of yellowish light. The sweet scent of the burning wax filled the room.

Tasha felt the quiet comfort of the place as she and the rest of the family walked down the carpeted aisle and took seats in the second row.

"I didn't expect the place to be so empty," Tasha

observed. Three people sat separately, facing the altar, their eyes closed.

"This isn't a regular service night," Miss Essie explained. "Try getting a seat in here on Sundays when Reverend Simon is preaching." She smiled fondly. "If he hadn't become a preacher, the man could have been an actor."

"I think Grandma has a crush on him," Allison teased.

"Hush up, girl," Miss Essie scolded, "before you find yourself teething on laundry soap."

"I turned in my report today," Allison whispered to Tasha.

"Good," her cousin said. "I'll keep my fingers crossed for you." Tasha leaned over close to Sarah. "It's been a long time since I've been in a church. What do I do?"

Tasha felt Sarah's hand gently squeeze her own.

"Just say what's on your mind, that's all," Sarah told her. "That's all you can do."

Tasha took a deep breath and leaned back against the hard wooden bench. She let the hush of the chapel close in on her. It was gentle, soothing.

To her right, Mr. and Mrs. Gordon sat gazing at the altar. They weren't saying anything, just holding hands and sitting.

Beyond them, Miss Essie had her eyes closed. Her left hand was gently fingering a small Bible. Tasha recognized it as one she had seen around the Gordon household. She probably knows every prayer by heart,

Tasha thought. Me? I can't even remember the one I used to say before I went to bed at night.

Allison sat next to her grandmother, and gazed around the chapel as if waiting for something miraculous to happen.

And Sarah, sitting to Tasha's left, had her hands folded in her lap. Her head was bowed and she was whispering so softly, Tasha could barely hear a sound.

Each in his or her own way, Tasha thought. *Say what's on your mind,* Sarah had said.

Slowly, tentatively, the words came to Tasha. She closed her eyes and raised her head to the stained-glass window just above the altar.

"Mom, Dad," she said softly. "There's so much I never told you. And so much you never said to me. I guess we all thought we had plenty of time.

"Mom, I'm sorry I didn't spend more time with you. I was so busy trying to get Daddy's attention—I guess I ignored yours. I love you, Mom.

"Daddy..." She choked back the words at first. "Where were you? I know you were making sure Mom and I never wanted for anything. But we did...we wanted you.

"I know you wanted to make your mom and dad proud of you," Tasha went on. She opened her eyes long enough to look at Miss Essie. "Know something though, I bet they always were proud of you. It was just hard for you to see that. I have the same problem sometimes. Maybe we are a lot alike.

"I miss you both," Tasha said, tears slowly running

down her face. "I wish you were going to be there when I graduate from college, or when ... well, if I get married." She paused and opened her eyes. "Then again, maybe you will be there in spirit."

She reached out and took Sarah's and her aunt's hands. They both held on tightly. "I'm with good people—good family, now. They want me, and I feel like I belong.

"Guess that's it ..." Tasha hesitated for a moment, then said, "If it's okay, from time to time, I might just start talking to you. Hope you can handle it up there. Down here, we're just fine."

PINE

Nineteen

"Sorry it took so long." Cindy and Sarah had been waiting for Tasha after school on Thursday. "Anna's in there playing one-on-one, and I wanted to see how she was making out."

"How is she doing?" Sarah asked.

"Okay," Tasha answered. "Still a little ragged around the edges, but okay."

"Hey, Tash—I guess I haven't been too cool lately," Cindy said. "I've been trying to think why I haven't been, but I haven't come up with anything. I just want to say I'm sorry."

"It just hurt like crazy when everybody started looking at me as if I did cheat on that test," Tasha said.

"We knew better," Cindy said. "Everybody in the school knows you're smart. Most of the teachers are on your side now."

"Not the point, girlfriend." Tasha held the door for Sarah and Cindy. "Where were you when I needed a friend? If I *had* cheated, if I *had* used a calculator, I still needed a friend."

They were outside and two of the yellow school buses were blocking the rear gate. Sarah nodded toward the road that cut past the athletic fields and they followed her.

"If you had cheated then you would have been wrong," Cindy said. "Right?"

"So that means as long as I'm perfect, you're my friend, but if I'm not—" Tasha took a deep breath. "If I do something that's wrong, then you and I are through?"

"I guess not," Cindy said.

"I hope not," Tasha came back, "because that doesn't make friendship all that good."

The three girls stopped and watched a basketball game between some freshman boys. A short, overweight boy was huffing and puffing his way around the court, guarding the other team with his left hand and holding up his pants with the other.

"I would say something about being friends through thick and thin," Sarah said, "but I was worse than anybody. How come we're so quick to get down on somebody if we think they're in trouble? All the good things we know about them seem to get crowded out."

"When an adult says something, we sort of listen to them more than if a kid said it," Cindy said.

As they walked past the court the ball rolled toward them and Cindy stopped it with her foot.

"Hey, pretty baby, throw the ball back!" one of the boys called to her.

Cindy nudged it with her foot in the opposite direction and gave the boy a smile.

"That was stupid!" the boy said as he chased the basketball.

Tasha suddenly thought about the driveway of her house in California. Seven years ago, she and her father had been playing one-on-one, just for the fun of it. They didn't do it often, but whenever they did, it was a time of energy and laughter. And when he wasn't around, she practiced so their next game would be even more exciting. She could see her father so clearly in her mind. His broad shoulders, his bright smile; his dancing eyes, her mother had always called them. How many shots did he let her have?

Tasha shook her head. "My dad and I used to play basketball. When he was home for a rest, or home games."

Sarah glanced from the game to Tasha. "Really? Is that where you learned?"

"Guess so."

"Did he play ball with you because he"—Cindy hesitated—"I mean, you know, because he wanted a son?"

Tasha chuckled softly. "No Cindy. It was just his

135

way." She thought for a moment. "And maybe he wanted me to be more competitive, like him. I don't know."

Sarah chuckled. "I wasn't that physical. When I was real young Mom, Dad, and I would wrestle in the backyard. But when I got older, we'd go for long walks, or Dad would take me to amusement parks and museums."

"I wish my dad did things like that with me." Cindy appeared to be brooding. "Back in Jamaica, when I was real little, I played on the beach with the other kids. And when we moved here—well, Dad is always working. When he gets home all he wants to do is eat and talk."

The girls strolled past the school and across the big lawn.

"How can boys be so different?" Cindy asked. "I mean look at the difference between Mr. Gordon, my dad, and yours, Tasha."

"I think it's a genes thing," Tasha offered.

"Too tight, or not tight enough?" Sarah said with a smile.

"Funny, cuz." Tasha noticed a curious expression on Cindy's face. "Something going on with more than one man in your life?"

Cindy shrugged. "Oh, it's just that Ibrahim tried to talk to me today. He says he's thinking of transferring out of Murphy."

"Why?" Sarah asked.

"He says that there's too much pressure on him here.

I think he's having trouble at home," Cindy explained. "But the way he acted you would think I did something to him."

"Well, later for him if he does go," Sarah said indifferently. She noticed Cindy was eyeing her with disapproval. "I'm sorry, but he's not going to get a whole lot of sympathy from me. You're my friend, Cindy, not him."

"I understand," Cindy replied. "Funny thing is I think I'm going to miss him."

"Until a new guy comes along," Tasha said.

"I didn't say I was going to mourn Ibrahim," Cindy said with a smile, "just miss him."

They strolled down Eastmont, heading in the general direction of 18 Pine.

"Did anybody hear what Kwame said in history the other day?" Sarah asked.

"What did he say?" Cindy asked.

"The teacher asked what was the most reliable way to world peace," Sarah answered. "Kwame raised his hand and said, 'Down Eastmont.' The teacher asked how going down Eastmont had anything to do with world peace. Kwame said 'Oh, world *peace*, I thought you said world *pizza*!'"

PINE

Twenty

The house was empty except for Tasha and Miss Essie, who was napping on the couch. When the doorbell rang, Tasha answered it and found Kwame standing in the doorway.

"I just came to pick up a book from Sarah," Kwame said. "She said she was going to leave it on the television."

"Come on in," Tasha said, leading him into the living room. A poetry anthology was sitting on the top of the television.

"What's this for, a book report?" Tasha asked.

"No, not really," Kwame said. He was obviously embarrassed.

"So what's it for?" Tasha said, pulling the book back from him.

"Hey, lighten up!" Kwame complained. "This is Special K, the new Kwame, you know. Poetry is just part of my total bag."

"Tell me what it's for," Tasha said. "Or you won't get it."

"It's going to be part of my new image," Kwame said. "Naomi said my old image was getting kind of tired."

"Naomi said that?" Tasha was surprised. "I didn't even know you and Naomi were that close."

"We're not anymore," Kwame said. "I blew it when she found out I couldn't kiss."

"Wait a minute," Tasha said. "You've been kissing Naomi, and she said you can't kiss? Is that what I'm hearing?"

"Yeah, I asked her if I could take her to the movies," Kwame said, "and she asked me if I could kiss."

"What did you say?"

"I said yes," Kwame said, "but then she told me to kiss her and I did."

"You kissed her and she dissed you?"

"So now I'm into poetry."

"How did you kiss her?" Tasha asked.

"You know, the regular way," Kwame said.

Tasha didn't know why she was going to kiss Kwame, but she knew she was going to. It had something to do with the idea that she liked him, and she had a perfect excuse. "Show me," she said.

Kwame looked down at the ground, and then away. "Yo, Tasha, you said we were just going to be friends," he said. "My heart can't stand but so much."

"So Naomi put you down and now you're going to put me down," Tasha said, feeling slightly wicked.

Kwame shrugged and moved closer.

As she put her arms around Kwame's neck, Tasha thought that she was badly in need of a kiss and *that* was why she was kissing him. She put everything she had into the kiss, too.

When they parted Kwame was breathing hard.

"You kiss fine," Tasha said.

"You do, too," Kwame said hoarsely.

"Get out of here, boy," Tasha said. "Before I put a *serious* hurting on your lips."

When Kwame had left, Tasha went into the kitchen and got a cold glass of water. She told herself that she shouldn't have been kissing Kwame. It just wasn't right. But it was soooo gooood!

The Gordon house was jumping when Tasha and Sarah arrived home from school on Friday. Voices were raised and Allison was jumping up and down.

"Did someone burn dinner again?" Sarah asked.

Allison ran over and hugged both Sarah and Tasha. "She said it was one of the most in-depth reports she had read this semester. She said I had stimulated her interest in a whole new list of poets and—"

141

"You got a good mark on your report!" Tasha exclaimed, hugging Allison close.

"She received an A-plus," Mr. Gordon announced proudly.

"That's great," Sarah cheered.

"A few kids did the same old stuff, but I—"

"I hope you told your teacher, Mrs. Conover, how inspiring your sister and your cousin were," Mrs. Gordon said.

"Well..." Allison seemed a little embarrassed. "I did say I had a little help researching."

"Thanks loads," Tasha teased. She dropped down in a chair next to the television.

"Well," Allison said, edging toward the hallway, "I mean, I did do all the writing. I would have found all the poets, too, but I knew how much you wanted to help."

Tasha and Sarah's eyes widened. "Why, you little—"

Allison was out the door and laughing as Tasha and Sarah took off after her.

Saturday morning began with Sarah and Allison tiptoeing into Tasha's room at eight.

Hidden underneath her covers, Tasha mumbled that she needed another half hour.

Then Allison lifted the blankets just enough to allow an aroma to reach her cousin. In the cozy darkness, Tasha immediately recognized the smells of toast, marmalade, eggs, and vegetables.

"Mushroom omelet!" Tasha exclaimed as she threw

back her covers.

Sarah set the tray on Tasha's lap. "We thought you'd like breakfast in bed for once."

"Don't get used to it," Allison grumbled as she placed the juice and toast on the tray. "I won't be doing this a lot."

"You have fifteen minutes for your dining pleasure," Sarah said. "Then you have to hustle."

"I've got to hustle where?" Tasha said.

"Dad's arranged a meeting with Mr. Cala," Sarah said.

"What's he going to do to him?"

"He told Mom that he wasn't going to do or say anything rash," Sarah said. "That's all we know."

"Where's the meeting?"

"Murphy High," Sarah said. "That's where we're going to get him."

"Who's we?"

"You'll see," Sarah said.

"But ..."

"But me no buts," Sarah went on. "Dad borrowed a friend's minivan. The family's going in that, and Cindy and the gang are riding with Billy and Dave. So hustle, girl. Hustle!"

PINE

Twenty–One

The ride to school was like a camp outing. Mrs. Gordon told about her most embarrassing date, which happened to have been her first date with Mr. Gordon.

For the rest of the ride they laughed, talked, and sang, avoiding the one topic that continued to flash through Tasha's mind—Mr. Cala, and what was going to be said.

Everyone piled out of the van and into the school. It was eerie to be in the building on a Saturday. They walked up two flights of stairs and stood outside a math classroom. Mr. Gordon turned to the family and said, "Tasha and I are going in. The rest of you wait out here. And keep your fingers crossed!"

"As your legal counsel, I'm going, too," Mrs. Gordon said.

"What shall I say to him, Uncle Donald?" Tasha asked as they stood in front of the classroom.

"Nothing," Mr. Gordon said. "I'll do the talking."

"Fine with me," Tasha said.

They walked into the room. Mr. Cala was already there, together with Mrs. Feder, head of the math department.

Mr. Cala looked at Tasha, and then at Mr. and Mrs. Gordon. His eyes narrowed behind his glasses. "Miss Gordon," he said, trying to put a smile in his voice. "How pleasant to see you."

"I'm sure it's pleasant to see all of us," Mr. Gordon said. "Sorry to disrupt your Saturday. We just wanted to have a formal meeting to let you know that we don't believe that Tasha was cheating on the math test."

"Well, your opinion is duly noted." Mr. Cala reddened.

"Perhaps it should be more than noted, Mr. Cala," Mrs. Gordon said. "Because we might have to challenge your accusations with a lawsuit."

Mr. Cala made a grunting noise.

Mr. Gordon said, "I just wanted to say to Tasha, in your presence, that I don't want her to worry about any vicious rumors she may have heard. Rumors are generally spread by the people who have the least ability to determine truth from lies. And they are usually believed by even weaker people."

Out of the corner of her eye Tasha saw Mr. Cala stiffen at the sound of her uncle's words.

"A mistake was made," Mrs. Gordon said. "But who-

146

ever made the mistake is only human, and we all make human mistakes. However, I assure you that should those rumors continue . . ."

"If they continue"—Mr. Gordon spoke the words slowly so that no one, especially Mr. Cala, would miss them—"the financial cost to those involved will be far greater than they can imagine. I think, Mr. Cala, that a formal apology is in order."

Mrs. Feder interrupted. "Mr. Cala, Mr. Gordon. I don't think that it is necessary for it to come to this. We're all members of the educational community, and I believe that this can be settled in an amicable fashion."

Mr. Cala appeared relieved that Mrs. Feder had taken over, and began to look smug again.

"I think we all agree that Mr. Cala made a serious mistake when he publicly accused Ms. Gordon of cheating," Mrs. Feder said. Mr. Cala turned red again. "And I'm embarrassed that many of my fellow teachers initially went along with him."

Tasha was surprised. She knew that many of the teachers had backed Mr. Cala, but it seemed as though Mrs. Feder had spoken to them. She was pleased that some of her other teachers were behind her.

"In fact," Mrs. Feder continued, "I have letters from every single one of Tasha's current teachers, telling me that they do not believe she cheated." Mrs. Feder held up a stack of letters. Mr. and Mrs. Gordon looked at each other and smiled.

"Tasha would never cheat—" Mr. Gordon started.

"Let's let Mrs. Feder finish," Mrs. Gordon said.

"Given the support from her family and teachers, together with the lack of proof in your charges, I think the best course of action would be for you to forgo a formal hearing and apologize to Tasha now," Mrs. Feder said to Mr. Cala.

Mr. Cala stiffened. His face turned bright red. He sputtered, then stared at the table. When he spoke, his voice was very low. "Miss Gordon, sometimes people make mistakes. It is obvious to me, from the support you are receiving from your family, friends, and—my colleagues"—he paused and looked out the window—"that you are innocent of cheating. You have my sincere apology."

Mr. Gordon stepped back just enough to let Mrs. Gordon and Tasha hug each other.

Tasha took her aunt's hand, smiled at Mrs. Feder, and walked out of the room, ignoring Mr. Cala. When she walked into the hall, she was overwhelmed.

Standing in the hallway was a crowd of nearly fifty people. Tasha could see Sarah, Cindy, April, Jennifer, Kwame, Brian, Billy, Anna, Naomi, and the rest of the basketball team. Behind them were more than a dozen teachers from Murphy, together with even more kids, some of whom she didn't know. Tasha gasped. She knew who her friends were now.

"Right on, Tasha!" Brian Wu called from across the crowd. "We're proud of you."

It seemed like a hundred voices congratulated her at once. There were hugs all around as Tasha led the group out of the school, leaving Mr. Cala far behind.

Twenty–Two

"I still don't believe it!" Kwame stretched himself over two seats in 18 Pine and took a bite out of a large slice of Sicilian pizza.

"You should have seen the look on his face," April said.

Sarah eagerly bit into a meatball calzone. "We stood up for what was right. And Mom was right. Mr. Cala made a mistake, but he's just human, and he has faults like the rest of us. Who knows? Maybe he'll change completely and be a really neat-o sweet-o pussycat."

"Maybe we'll all change a little," Brian said. "It was easy for me to believe you cheated because I was sure that I was going to do better than you, Tasha."

149

"Hey, Brian, I bet I can beat you one-on-one in basketball, too," Tasha said.

"Hey, no way," Brian said.

"Why not?"

"Well, you know, you're a girl."

There was a collective moan and Brian realized what he had said. He went off to the counter and ordered enough pizza to quiet everyone down.

"With extra pepperoni, Brian," April called, "and maybe we'll forgive you."

Coming in Book 5, Sky Man

"Sky's off the team," Dave said, clearly upset.

"What did he do?" Sarah asked.

"The coach benched him for bad grades. His SAT scores were lousy, and now it looks like he's failing history, too. We were on our way to the state championships, but now it looks like we'll never make it."

"So what are we going to do?" Jennifer asked. "We can't let his career go down the drain."

When Sky, a hot basketball player on his way to the pros, transfers to Murphy, everyone's excited. Dave's glad to see the team win, Jennifer has found a new guy, and the school is buzzing.

But is Sky everything he seems to be? Sarah's not sure he can read, but Sky refuses her help, and the teachers seem willing to pass him even if he doesn't come to class.

Is it too late for Murphy? Too late for Sky?